A Background Note about *The Beasts of Tarzan*

The Beasts of Tarzan is the third book in the Tarzan series. The story begins in 1912 with Tarzan—now John Clayton, Lord Greystoke—in the Paris apartment of his friend, Paul D'Arnot. If you have not read the first two Tarzan books, you may wonder how Tarzan has gone from being the ape-man to Lord Greystoke. Some background may help:

In *Tarzan of the Apes*, Tarzan's parents die while in Africa, and their infant son is adopted by a tribe of apes. Tarzan then grows into the strong "king of the jungle." As a young man, he encounters the beautiful Jane Porter and William Cecil Clayton, Tarzan's own cousin and the supposed heir to the Greystoke fortune. Tarzan saves Jane's life and falls in love with her but believes she loves Cecil. At the end, Tarzan learns that he is the true heir to the Greystoke fortune, but keeps the secret to himself so that Cecil and Jane might enjoy the Greystoke money. We are left wondering if Jane is secretly in love with Tarzan.

At the start of the second book, *The Return of Tarzan*, Tarzan is heartsick and lonely. He goes to Paris to spend time with his friend D'Arnot. He is caught in a whirlwind of intrigues, and the evil Nikolai Rokoff becomes his enemy. A secret mission then takes Tarzan back to his African home. While he is there, a shipwreck strands Jane, Cecil, and Rokoff nearby. As Cecil dies of fever, Jane learns of Tarzan's true identity. She declares her love for Tarzan and the two are married. Rokoff is arrested and taken to face justice in France. At the end, Tarzan and Jane—now Lord and Lady Greystoke—set sail for England to settle down and start a family.

EDGAR RICE BURROUGHS
THE BEASTS OF TARZAN

Edited, and with an Afterword,
by Jonathan Kelley

TP THE TOWNSEND LIBRARY

THE BEASTS OF TARZAN

TP THE TOWNSEND LIBRARY

For more titles in the Townsend Library,
visit our website: **www.townsendpress.com**

All new material in this edition is
copyright © 2004 by Townsend Press.
Printed in the United States of America

0 9 8 7 6 5 4 3 2 1

Townsend Press, Inc.
1038 Industrial Drive
West Berlin, New Jersey 08091

ISBN 1-59194-033-8

Library of Congress Control Number:
2004105873

CONTENTS

1

Kidnapped

"The entire affair is mysterious," said D'Arnot. "Neither the police nor the military investigators have the faintest idea how it happened. All that anyone knows is that Nikolai Rokoff has escaped."

John Clayton, Lord Greystoke—who had been "Tarzan of the Apes"—sat in silence in the apartment of his friend, Lieutenant Paul D'Arnot, in Paris. The escape brought back many memories, for the ape-man's testimony had sent his archenemy to a French prison for life. Rokoff had gone to great lengths to try to kill Tarzan before, and having escaped, would likely now try twice as hard.

Tarzan had recently brought his wife and infant son to London to get away from the rainy season on their vast estates in Uziri—the land of the fierce Waziri warriors whose broad African domains the ape-man had once ruled. He had just arrived to visit D'Arnot, but the news about Rokoff made him want to return immediately to London.

"I do not fear for myself, Paul," he said at last.

"Rokoff has tried and failed many times to kill me. But he knows that he could hurt me most through my son or my wife. I must return to guard them until Rokoff is recaptured—or dead."

As these two talked in Paris, two dark, sinister-looking men were talking in a little cottage on the outskirts of London. One was bearded; the other had only a few days' growth, and his face was pale from long confinement indoors. He spoke:

"You must shave off that beard of yours, Alexei," he told his companion, "or he will recognize you immediately. We must split up, and when we meet again on the deck of the *Kincaid*, hopefully we shall have with us two honored guests who have no idea of the pleasant voyage we have arranged for them. In two hours I should be on my way to Dover with one of them. By tomorrow night, if all goes as planned, you should arrive with the other."

Alexei Paulvitch nodded.

"This will be profitable and satisfying, my dear Alexei. The French were stupid to conceal my escape for so long; they gave me plenty of time to work out every detail. There is very little chance that anything will go wrong. And now good-bye, and good luck!"

Three hours later, a messenger climbed the steps to the apartment of Lieutenant D'Arnot.

"A telegram for Lord Greystoke," he said to the servant who answered the door. "Is he here?"

The servant answered 'yes,' signed for the message, and took it to Tarzan, who was already preparing to depart for London. The ape-man tore open the envelope. As he read the message, his face went white.

"Read it, Paul," he said, handing the slip of paper to D'Arnot. "It has come already."

The Frenchman took the telegram and read:

Jack stolen from the garden with help of new servant. Come at once.

— JANE

As Tarzan leaped from the car that had met him at the station and ran up the steps to his London town house, he was met at the door by his frantic wife. Quickly Jane Porter Clayton, Lady Greystoke, told all that she had learned of the boy's kidnapping.

The baby's nurse had been wheeling him in the stroller, in front of the house. A taxicab had pulled up, and almost immediately the new house-servant, Carl, had come running from the house to tell the nurse that Lady Greystoke wanted to speak with her inside. He would watch little Jack until she returned. The nurse went, but at the top of the stairs, she turned to remind Carl not to let the sun get in the baby's eyes.

When she did so, she had been horrified to see Carl handing the baby to a dark-bearded stranger inside the cab. As she ran shrieking down to the vehicle, Carl jumped into the cab. While the driver tried to get it into gear, the frantic nurse jumped onto the running board, trying to reach in and grab the baby. As the cab finally got under way, Carl had slugged the nurse in the face and knocked her to the pavement. The vehicle sped off.

Her screams had attracted onlookers, including some from the Greystoke home. Lady Greystoke had witnessed the girl's brave battle, and had also tried to reach the rapidly accelerating vehicle, but had been too late.

That was all that anyone knew. Lady Greystoke had no idea who might be responsible until her husband told her of Rokoff's escape from prison.

As Tarzan and his wife considered what to do, the telephone rang in the library. Tarzan quickly answered it.

"Lord Greystoke?" asked a man's voice.

"Yes."

"Your son has been stolen," continued the voice, "and only I can help you recover him. I am familiar with the plot to kidnap him, for I was involved in it. They are now trying to cheat me out of my share of the reward. To get back at them, I will help you get your son back on one condition: that you will not prosecute me for my part in the crime. What do you say?"

"If you lead me to where my son is hidden," replied the ape-man, "you need fear nothing from me."

"Good," replied the other. "But you must come alone to meet me. I cannot take any chances."

"Where and when may I meet you?" asked Tarzan.

The caller gave the name and location of a sailors' bar on the waterfront at Dover. "Come alone, about ten o'clock tonight," he concluded. "Do not arrive earlier. Your son will be safe enough in the meantime, and I can then lead you secretly to where he is hidden. Under no circumstances notify Scotland Yard, or I will know. If you bring anyone else, or if I see anyone suspicious, I shall not meet you, and you will never get your son back."

The man hung up without another word.

Tarzan told Jane what the caller had said. She begged to go with him, but he insisted that she stay home, reminding her that the man had said he must come alone. She reluctantly agreed. Tarzan left immediately for Dover while she waited at home, impatient to learn the outcome of his mission.

Little did either dream of what either would experience before they saw each other again.

After her husband had left, Jane Clayton paced restlessly across the silken rugs of the library. She was a mother, deprived of her firstborn, and her mind and heart ached with hopes and fears. Though reason told her that all would be well provided her husband went alone as directed, she sensed that they were both in grave danger.

As she fretted, she began to believe that the phone call was likely just a trick to keep them from alerting the police until the boy was safely hidden away—or gotten out of England.

Or maybe it had been a trap to lure Tarzan into the hands of the hateful Rokoff.

This was a terrifying thought, but it made sense. She glanced up at the clock in the library; it was too late to catch Tarzan's train to Dover, but there was a later train that would get her there in time. Jane summoned her maid and chauffeur, and ten minutes later she was being whisked through the crowded streets toward the railway station.

It was 9:45 that night when Tarzan entered the squalid waterfront pub. As he entered the evil-smelling room a muffled figure brushed past him toward the street.

"Come, my lord!" whispered the stranger.

The ape-man turned to follow him into the dark alley. Once outside, the fellow led the way into the shadows of the high-piled bales, boxes, and barrels on the wharf. Here he halted.

"Where is the boy?" asked Greystoke.

"On that small steamer whose lights you can just see yonder," replied the other.

Tarzan was trying to recognize the man, but the darkness prevented it. Had he guessed that it was Alexei Paulvitch, he would have realized that only treachery and danger lurked ahead.

"He is unguarded now," continued the Russian. "The kidnappers think no one can find them, and the only members of the *Kincaid's* crew aboard have been given enough gin to keep them occupied for several hours. We can go aboard, get the child, and return without the slightest fear."

Tarzan nodded. "Let's be about it, then," he said.

His guide led him to a small boat by the dock. The two men got in, and Paulvitch rowed rapidly toward the steamer. At the time, Tarzan did not notice the black smoke pouring from the *Kincaid's* funnel; he thought only of the hope that in a few moments he would again have his little son in his arms.

At the steamer's side they found a rope ladder dangling close above them, and both climbed stealthily up it. Once on deck they hastened aft to where the Russian pointed to a hatch.

"The boy is hidden there," he said. "You had better go down alone to get him. There is less chance that he will cry in fright in his father's arms. I will stand guard here."

In his anxiety to rescue little Jack, Tarzan did not consider the strangeness of the whole picture. The ship's deck was deserted, but its engines were thrumming and smoke was rising from the funnel—sure signs of a vessel about to sail. Intent on recovering the precious little bundle of humanity, the ape-man swung down into the darkness below.

Scarcely had he let go of the edge of the hatch when it fell shut with a clatter.

Instantly he knew that it had been a trap. Instead of rescuing his son, he had himself fallen into the hands of his enemies. He immediately tried to push the hatch open, but it would not budge. He struck a match and looked around. He discovered that he was in a little compartment separated from the main hold. The hatch was the only way in or out of the empty chamber. If the child was aboard, he was in another part of the ship.

For over twenty years, from infancy to manhood, the ape-man had roamed his savage jungle haunts among the beasts. He had never learned to rage over a bad situation, as humans do. Like an animal, he simply waited patiently while trying to figure a way out. He examined his prison carefully, tested the heavy planking of its walls, and measured the distance of the hatch above.

As he did so, he suddenly felt the ship move. Where—and to what fate—was it carrying him? Then, over the noise of the engines, he heard a sound that make his blood run cold with worry.

Clear and shrill from the deck above him rang the scream of a frightened woman.

2

Marooned

As Tarzan and his guide were disappearing into the shadows on the dock, a heavily veiled woman hurried down the narrow alley to the entrance of the pub they had just left.

She paused, looked around to be sure she had the right place, and pushed bravely inside. More than a dozen half-drunken sailors and dock-rats looked up at the unusual sight of a richly gowned woman in their midst. She strode rapidly toward the barmaid.

"Have you seen a tall, well-dressed man here just a minute ago," she asked, "who met another and went away with him?"

"I have, milady, but where they went I've no idea," she replied. A nearby sailor offered more information: just outside the pub, he had seen two men leaving it in the direction of the docks.

"Show me where they went," cried the woman, slipping a coin into the man's hand.

The fellow led her outside and along the wharf. Across the water they saw a small boat disappearing into the shadow of a nearby steamer.

"There they are," whispered the man.

"I'll give you ten pounds if you will find a boat and row me to that steamer," cried the woman.

"Quick, then," he replied, "if we're goin' to catch the *Kincaid* afore she sails. She's had steam up for three hours, one of her crew told me, jest a-waitin' fer that one passenger." As he spoke, he led her to a boat and helped her into it, then jumped in and pushed off. Soon they were headed across the water.

At the steamer's side the man demanded his pay. The woman thrust a handful of money into his outstretched hand. He glanced down, saw that he had been well paid, and helped her onto the ladder. He kept the boat alongside, in case she might wish to be taken ashore later. But presently he heard the sounds of the *Kincaid's* anchor being raised, and a moment later he heard the propellers. Slowly the little steamer moved out into the channel.

As he turned to row back to shore he heard a woman's shriek from the ship's deck. He shrugged and began to row back toward the dock.

When Jane Clayton reached the deck, no one was in sight. Hoping against hope, she hastened to the main cabin structure in search of her husband and child. She hurried down the short ladder into the main cabin. Along both sides of this room were the doors to the officers' quarters. In her hurry, she did not notice that one of those doors that had been open was quickly closed.

She passed the full length of the main room, then retraced her steps to listen at each door and quietly try its latch. It was so silent she could feel the beating of her frightened heart. One by one the doors opened before her touch, only to reveal empty rooms. She was too absorbed to note the sudden sounds of the engines getting under way.

She had reached the last door on the right now, and as she pushed it open she was seized from within by a powerful, dark-bearded man who drew her hastily into the stuffy interior. The sudden fright drew a single piercing scream from her throat before the man clapped a hand roughly over her mouth.

"Not until we are farther from land, my dear," he said. "Then you may yell your pretty head off."

Lady Greystoke turned to look into the leering, bearded face. The man relaxed the pressure of his fingers on her lips, and with a little moan of recognition and terror she shrank away from her captor.

"Nikolai Rokoff!" she exclaimed.

"Your devoted admirer," replied the Russian, with a low bow.

"My little boy—where is he? Let me have him! Even you, Nikolai Rokoff, cannot be so merciless! Tell me—is he on this ship? Oh, please, take me to my baby!"

"If you do as you are told no harm will come to him," replied Rokoff. "But remember that it is your own fault that you are here, so you shall take the consequences. I little expected such good luck." He then locked her in the cabin and went on deck.

While she was imprisoned in the cabin, her only visitor was the *Kincaid's* messy cook, Sven Anderssen. He was a tall raw-boned Swede with a long yellow complexion and filthy nails. The very sight of him with one grimy thumb buried deep in the lukewarm stew—the only thing he ever brought her—was enough to ruin her appetite. He was a shifty, catlike man with a long slim knife at his waist, which Jane suspected was not merely a kitchen tool. His manner toward her was surly, but she always smiled and thanked him when he brought her food. Usually, she hurled it out the porthole as soon as he left.

During the following days of anguish, she could think only of her husband and son. She believed the baby was aboard—if he was still living—but whether Tarzan had been left alive after having been lured aboard the evil craft she could not guess. Rokoff hated her husband for having thwarted many of his plans, and especially for causing him to be sent to prison. The only logical motive for Rokoff to bring Tarzan aboard would be murder.

Tarzan, in fact, lay in the darkness of his cell, ignorant of the fact that his wife was a prisoner in the cabin almost above his head.

Anderssen also brought Tarzan's meals to him, but the ape-man was unable to strike up a conversation with him. He had hoped to learn through the cook whether his little son was aboard the *Kincaid*, but always the fellow repeated the same reply: "Ay tink it blow purty soon purty hard." After several attempts Tarzan gave up.

For weeks the little steamer forged on, its destination unknown to the prisoners. Once the *Kincaid* stopped to refuel and then got moving again. The weeks felt like months to Tarzan and Jane.

Rokoff had visited Jane Clayton only once since he had locked her away. He had been thin and hollow-eyed, in a foul temper from a long bout of seasickness. "It is now time for us to do business," began the Russian. "If you wish safe return to England, you will write me a check in the amount I require." He named an outrageous sum.

"When you set me down safely in any civilized port, together with my son and my husband," she replied, "I will pay you in gold twice the amount you ask; but otherwise I will not give you a cent."

"You will give me what I ask," he replied with a snarl, "or neither you nor your child nor your husband will ever again set foot in any port, civilized or otherwise."

"Why should I trust you?" she replied. "What guarantee do I have that you will not take my money and then do as you please anyway?"

"I think you will do it," he said, turning to leave the cabin. "Remember that I have your son. If you hear the wail of a tortured child, you can enjoy the knowledge that your baby is suffering because of your own stubbornness."

"You could not be so fiendishly cruel!" she cried.

"You are the cruel one," he returned. "You will let your baby suffer, all because of a little money."

In the end, Jane Clayton wrote out a large check and handed it to Nikolai Rokoff, who left her cabin with an evil grin of satisfaction.

The following day the hatch of Tarzan's cell opened. He looked up to see Paulvitch's head framed against the sky.

"Come up," commanded the Russian. "One hostile move and you will be shot."

The ape-man swung himself lightly to the deck. Surrounding him at a respectful distance stood a half-dozen sailors armed with rifles and revolvers. Facing him was Paulvitch.

Tarzan looked around for Rokoff, who must surely be aboard, but there was no sign.

"Lord Greystoke," Paulvitch began, "your continued interference with Monsieur Rokoff and his plans has gotten you and your family into this. It has cost him a great deal of money, and he rightfully considers that you owe him repayment. What is more, only by meeting Monsieur Rokoff's reasonable demands can you save your wife, your child, and yourself."

"How much?" asked Tarzan. "And how do I know that you will keep your bargain? I have little reason to trust a scoundrel such as you."

The Russian flushed. "You are in no position to insult me," he said. "You have only my word. And I give you my word on another thing: if you do not write the check we demand, we will make short work of you. You might be a fool, but you know enough to realize what pleasure it would give me to order these men to fire. We only refrain from shooting you because it would ruin our other plans for punishing you."

"Answer one question," said Tarzan. "Is my son on board this ship?"

"No," replied Alexei Paulvitch, "your son is quite safe elsewhere, and he will not be killed unless you refuse our fair demands. If we have to kill you, the child will be only a needless risk for us, one we would eliminate. Therefore, you can only save his life by saving your own, and you can only do that by writing us the check."

"Very well," replied Tarzan, for Paulvitch's word was good on at least one point: they would surely carry out any evil threat they made. There was a bare chance that giving in to their demands might save the boy. He assumed they would not allow him to live after he signed the check, but he would give them a battle they would never forget. He might even take Paulvitch down with him; too bad it was not Rokoff.

He took his checkbook and fountain pen from his pocket.

"What is the amount?" he asked. Paulvitch named an enormous sum.

Tarzan could barely restrain a smile. Their own greed had ruined their plans, at least with regard to the ransom, for there was nowhere near that amount in his bank account. The ape-man made a show of haggling and complaining over the amount, but Paulvitch would not budge. Finally the ape-man sullenly wrote out a check he knew would bounce.

As he turned to hand the worthless slip of paper to the Russian, he happened to look across the starboard bow. To his surprise, the ship was a few hundred yards from land. A dense tropical jungle ran almost down to the water's edge.

Paulvitch noted the direction of his gaze. "You are to be released here," he said.

Tarzan's plan for immediate physical revenge vanished. The land before him must be Africa. Africa had been his first home; he could easily find his way back to civilization.

Paulvitch took the check. "Remove your clothing," he said to the ape-man. "You will not need it."

Tarzan hesitated. Paulvitch pointed to the armed sailors, and the ape-man slowly did as ordered. A boat was lowered, and Tarzan was rowed ashore under heavy guard. Half an hour later the sailors had returned to the *Kincaid*, and soon Tarzan stood on the beach watching the vessel recede. The ape-man was about to read a note one of the sailors had given him when he looked up at the ship. He saw a black-bearded man appear at the rail and call out to him. The man was laughing scornfully and holding high above his head the tiny figure of a baby.

Tarzan nearly started to rush through the surf and swim for the already moving steamer, but he realized the futility of this and halted at the water's edge. Instead he stood, watching the *Kincaid* until it disappeared beyond a small peninsula.

From the jungle at his back, fierce bloodshot eyes glared at him from beneath shaggy overhanging brows. Little monkeys chattered and scolded, and from far inland came the scream of a leopard, but John Clayton, Lord Greystoke, paid no heed. He was consumed with regret that he had been fool enough to believe anything told him by his archenemy's main henchman.

"At least Jane is safe in London," he thought. "Thank heaven, she did not fall into the clutches of those villains."

Behind him, the hairy thing was creeping stealthily toward him.

Where were the trained senses of the savage ape-man?

Where the acute hearing?

Where the uncanny sense of scent?

3

Beasts at Bay

Slowly Tarzan unfolded and read the note the sailor had handed him. It took a few moments for the full impact of the hideous plot of revenge to strike him. The note read:

These are my plans for you and your son.

You were born an ape, naked in the jungle, and an ape you remain. Your son shall rise above his animal father: he shall wear a loincloth and copper anklets, perhaps even a ring in his nose, for he is to be raised by a tribe of savages.

I might have killed you, but that would have been too lenient. Instead, you will live the rest of your life knowing your son's fate and knowing that you cannot help him.

This is but part of your punishment for having dared to oppose me.

N.R.

P.S. The rest of your punishment has to do with your wife. I leave her fate to your imagination.

As he finished reading, a slight sound behind him brought his senses back to reality. He was again Tarzan of the Apes, a beast at bay, ready to fight for his life against the charging bull-ape who bore down on him.

In the past three years, Tarzan's great abilities had only slightly faded. His life on his vast estate in Uziri had kept him in practice. Even at his peak, though, he would never have welcomed unarmed battle with this shaggy, bull-necked beast—but he had no choice.

Over the bull's shoulder Tarzan could see the heads and shoulders of a dozen more apes. Fortunately for Tarzan, apes were not intelligent enough to gang up on an enemy, otherwise they would have come to dominate the jungle with their powerful muscles and fangs.

With a low snarl, the beast now hurled himself at Tarzan, but this was a different Tarzan than the one who left the jungle three years earlier. He had learned new tactics. The charge that he would once have met with brute force, he now side-stepped. As the beast hurtled past, Tarzan swung a mighty right to the pit of the ape's stomach.

With a howl of mingled rage and anguish, the great ape bent double and sank to the ground, then struggled to rise again. Before he could, his human foe had wheeled to pounce on him, and in that last act the final shred of the cloak of civilization dropped from the shoulders of the English lord. Once again he was Tarzan, son of Kala the she-ape, reveling in bloody conflict with his kind.

His strong, white teeth sank into the hairy

throat of his enemy as he sought the pulsing jugular. Powerful fingers held the mighty fangs from his own flesh, and when possible, became fists to punch the snarling, foam-flecked face with the power of a steam-hammer.

The rest of the apes stood about them in a circle, enjoying the struggle. They muttered low grunts of approval as bits of white hide or hairy bloodstained skin were torn from one contestant or the other. But they were silent in amazement when they saw the mighty white ape climb onto their king's back, slip steel muscles beneath his enemy's armpits, and bear down mightily with his open palms upon the back of the thick neck. The ape-king could only shriek in agony and flounder helplessly about on the ground; Tarzan had him in the same hold—the full nelson—that he had once discovered by accident in battle with the huge Terkoz. The ape-audience heard the creaking of their king's neck mingling with his agonized shrieks and roars.

Then there came a sudden *crack!*, like a tree-limb breaking in a high wind. The bullet-head crumpled forward against the great hairy chest, and the roaring and the shrieking ceased. The watching apes' pig-like little eyes wandered from the still form of their leader to that of the white ape, then back to their fallen king.

The newcomer stood and placed a foot upon the neck of the silent figure at his feet. Then he threw back his head and vented a sound they knew well: the wild challenge of the bull-ape over a kill. Their king was dead.

The horrid notes of the victory-cry tore through the jungle. The little monkeys in the tree-tops ceased their chattering. The noisy, brilliant-plumed birds were still. From afar came the answering wail of Sheeta, the leopard, and the deep roar of Numa, the lion.

It was the old Tarzan who turned questioning eyes toward the little knot of apes before him. It was the old Tarzan who shook his head as though to clear long hair from his face—an old habit dating from when it had hung to his shoulders.

The ape-man knew what was next: an immediate attack from whichever surviving bull-ape now wished to be king. It was not unusual among the apes for a complete stranger to enter a community, kill the king, and take over the leadership. He could assume that role himself, but he was not sure he wanted the irksome duties of the job.

The decision was not left entirely up to Tarzan. A huge, splendidly muscled younger ape was edging threateningly closer to the ape-man. A low, sullen growl issued from between his bared fangs.

Tarzan stood like a statue, watching his every move. A single step backward would have incited a charge. Had he instead charged the young bull, the belligerent creature might either have fought or retreated, depending on his courage. To wait, perfectly still, was the middle course.

The bull followed the apes' custom: he approached quite close and circled slowly, growling and baring his fangs, just as Tarzan had expected. It might be a bluff, but an ape's mind is unstable. Any impulse might suddenly hurl the hairy mass upon the man, bashing and tearing.

Tarzan turned slowly to keep his eyes locked with those of the circling ape. This was likely a young bull who had not quite felt ready to overthrow his old king, but who would one day have done so. He was a big one, over seven feet tall with great, hairy arms reaching almost to the ground. His fighting fangs, now quite close to Tarzan's face, were exceptionally long and sharp. Like the others of his tribe, he looked slightly different from the apes of Tarzan's boyhood, so this could not be his former tribe.

As the threatening bull continued circling the ape-man, Tarzan decided to see if this tribe spoke the same language as that of Kerchak:

"Who are you," he asked, "who threatens Tarzan of the Apes?"

The hairy brute looked surprised. "I am Akut," replied the other in the same simple, basic tongue. "Molak is dead. I am king. Go away or I shall kill you!"

"You saw how easily I killed Molak," replied the ape-man. "Tarzan of the Apes could kill you as easily, if he cared to be king, but he does not wish to rule the tribe of Akut. All he wishes is to live in peace in this country. Let us be friends. Tarzan of the Apes can help you, and you can help Tarzan of the Apes."

"You cannot kill Akut," replied the other, his vigilance relaxing a bit. "None is so great as Akut. Had you not killed Molak, Akut would have done so, for Akut was ready to be king."

The ape-man answered this by hurling himself upon the great brute. He seized Akut's wrist, whirled him about, and leaped upon his broad back before the other had time to react. Down they went together, but Tarzan's move had worked. Before they struck the ground, he had Akut in the same hold that had broken Molak's neck. Slowly he increased the pressure.

And then, as he had once given Kerchak the chance to surrender and live, he allowed Akut to choose his fate: live in peace with Tarzan—perhaps even as a powerful ally—or die here and now, as he had just seen his once-invincible leader die.

"Ka-goda?" whispered Tarzan to the ape beneath him.

It was the same question that he had whispered to Kerchak, and it means: "Do you surrender?"

Akut thought of the creaking sound he had heard just before Molak's thick neck had snapped, and he shuddered. He hated to give up the king-ship, though, so again he struggled to free himself and got only more pressure on his neck. Suddenly, the pain was too awful—it brought an agonized "ka-goda!" from his lips.

Tarzan relaxed his grip.

"You may still be king, Akut," he said. "Tarzan told you that he did not wish to be king. If any question your right, Tarzan of the Apes will help you in your battles."

The ape-man rose and Akut came slowly to his feet. Shaking his bullet-like head and growling angrily, he waddled toward his tribe, looking to see if any of the larger bulls would challenge his leadership. None did; instead, they drew away as he approached, and presently the whole pack moved off into the jungle. Tarzan was left alone once more upon the beach. He was sore from the wounds that Molak had given him, but he endured the pain with the calm of a wild beast.

First he needed weapons. The confrontation with the apes, and the voices of Numa and Sheeta, made it obvious that life here would be neither easy nor secure. As in his old existence, there would be the constant bloodshed and danger of hunting—and being hunted. He would draw upon the ingenious craftsmanship he had learned from the Waziri, whose weapons he knew so well.

Along the shore he found an outcropping of shiny, brittle, black obsidian. With much effort, he managed to chip off a narrow sliver of the rock some twelve inches long by a quarter of an inch thick. One edge was quite thin near the tip: the beginning of a knife.

With it he went into the jungle, searching until he found a certain type of fallen tree. From this he cut a small straight branch, then sharpened one end of it. Next he scooped a small, round hole in the trunk, and crumbled bits of dry bark into it. Sitting on the fallen tree, he rolled the slender stick rapidly between his hands with its point in the hole.

After a time a thin wisp of smoke rose from the little mass of tinder, then became flame. Heaping larger twigs and sticks on the tiny fire, Tarzan soon had a respectable blaze roaring. He held the blade of his stone knife in the fire until it was very hot, then took it out and put a drop of moisture near the edge. The area beneath the droplet flaked away from the glassy blade, leaving a very sharp edge at that spot. He repeated this, each time at a new spot on the obsidian, until he had a cutting edge of a couple of inches; the rest he would finish later.

With that edge he made a long bow, a handle for his knife, a stout club and a supply of arrows. These he hid in a tall tree beside a little stream, and here also he built a platform with a roof of palm-leaves. By the time he finished, it was dusk, and Tarzan was hungry.

During his brief trip into the forest, he had noticed a watering hole a slight distance upstream from his tree, with many fresh tracks. To this spot the hungry ape-man made his silent way through the upper terrace of the jungle, swinging with the grace and ease of a monkey.

Although he felt sorrow over the loss of his family, he found pleasure in returning to the free life of his youth. He fell easily back into the old habits that were more a part of him than the thin veneer of civilization gained from his past three years living as Lord Greystoke. If only his fellows in the House of Lords could have seen him!

Silently he crouched in the lower branches of a great tree overhanging the trail, watching and listening alertly. He did not have long to wait. Just as he was getting comfortable, Bara, the deer, came daintily down to drink.

But more than Bara was coming. Behind the graceful buck came another hunter, which the deer could neither see nor scent. Tarzan could not yet see the hunter, but it was probably stalking Bara for the same reason as he. Numa, perhaps, or Sheeta, the panther.

In any event, if Bara did not hurry, Tarzan's meal would soon slip away.

As he had this thought, the buck heard the stalker make some noise. With a sudden start, he paused, trembled, then bounded straight for the river where Tarzan lurked above. If he could reach the stream, he would cross it and escape.

Now Tarzan saw the stalker plainly: Numa,

the lion. Bara would soon pass below. Could Tarzan pull it off? But even as he asked himself the question, the ape-man acted. He leaped from his perch and landed directly on the back of the startled buck.

In another instant Numa would be upon them both, so if the ape-man were to dine that night— or ever again—he must act quickly. His weight knocked Bara to his knees, and he grasped a great antler in either hand. With a single quick wrench he twisted the buck's neck completely around and felt it break. He then swung the deer across his shoulder just as the lion was closing in on him with roars of rage. Taking a foreleg in his strong teeth, Tarzan leaped for a low branch and hauled himself and his prey just out of reach of Numa's spring. The cruel talons slashed only air, and the baffled cat fell back to earth.

Then Tarzan of the Apes took his dinner up to the safety of a higher limb and grinned down into the gleaming yellow eyes of the other wild beast. Cutting into the deer's flank, he flung droplets of blood to taunt the cheated, infuriated Numa. He then cut a juicy venison steak, and in full view of the growling, pacing lion, feasted upon the tender flesh of his kill.

And so Lord Greystoke dined. No meal in the fanciest London club had ever tasted better. The warm blood of his kill smeared his hands and face, filling his nostrils with the favorite scent of the savage meat-eater.

When he had finished, he left the rest of the carcass in a high fork of the tree. With Numa trailing below him, still eager for revenge, he made his way back to his treetop shelter to sleep well into the following morning.

4

Sheeta

Tarzan spent the next few days completing his weapons and exploring the jungle. He strung his bow with Bara's tendons; they would do until he found the best bowstring material—the gut of Sheeta, the panther.

He also braided a long grass rope of the sort that he had long ago used to annoy the ill-natured Tublat. Such a rope had become a very effective weapon in the ape-boy's skilled hands. The hide and bones of Bara provided him with a sheath and better handle for his hunting knife, a quiver for arrows, and a belt and loincloth.

Then he set out to explore. This land was certainly not the familiar West African coast, for it faced east; the rising sun came up out of the sea here. Nor could it be the east coast of Africa, because the *Kincaid* had not been at sea long enough to reach it. It could not be some wild South American shore, for he knew that there were no lions there. He had no idea where he was.

As Tarzan made his lonely way through the

jungle along the shore, he began to regret not joining up with the apes. He had not seen them since the first day. Now he was nearly the Tarzan of old, and while he realized how little he had in common with Akut's tribe, they were better than being alone. His pace was slow, alternating between the ground and the lower branches, foraging for fruit and bugs, which he still found tasty.

Tarzan had covered a mile or more when to his delight he scented Sheeta upwind ahead of him. Not only would the great cat's strong gut make an excellent bowstring, his hide would make a new quiver and loincloth. The ape-man moved silently as he tracked the savage cat through the forest.

As he came closer to Sheeta, he realized that the panther was also stalking game. Soon his nostrils caught the strong musk of a group of great apes. He lost sight of Sheeta briefly but soon spotted the panther again—the big cat had climbed into a large tree. Beyond and below Sheeta lazed the tribe of Akut in a little clearing; some dozed against tree-trunks, while others foraged for grubs and beetles.

Akut was the closest to Sheeta. The cat crouched upon a thick limb, hidden from the ape's view by dense foliage, waiting patiently until his quarry was in range.

Tarzan cautiously moved into the same tree, a little above the panther, his slim obsidian blade in his left hand. He would have preferred to use his noose, but the foliage surrounding the huge cat made an accurate throw unlikely.

Akut had now wandered quite close beneath the tree that held his waiting death. Sheeta slowly edged his hind paws along the branch, and then with an awful shriek he began to launch himself toward the great ape. A fraction of a second before this, another beast of prey above him leaped, its own savage cry mingling with his.

As the startled Akut looked up, he saw the panther almost above him. On the panther's back was the white ape that had defeated him before near the great water.

The teeth of the ape-man were buried in the back of Sheeta's neck and his right arm was round the fierce throat, while the left hand brought a piece of stone up and down in mighty blows on the panther's side behind the shoulder.

Akut had just time to leap to one side to avoid being pinned beneath the battling monsters as they crashed to earth at his feet. Sheeta was screaming, snarling, and roaring horribly; but the white ape clung stubbornly to his thrashing quarry. The stone knife was driven home through the glossy hide over and over again, until with a final agonized lunge and shriek the great feline rolled over on its side and lay still.

Then the ape-man stood over his kill, raised his head, and once again his savage victory challenge rang through the jungle.

Akut and his apes stood looking in startled

wonder at the dead body of Sheeta and the lithe, straight figure of the man who had slain him.

Tarzan was the first to speak. He had saved Akut's life for a purpose, and he knew that he must make it clear to the ape.

"I am Tarzan of the Apes," he said, "mighty hunter and mighty fighter. By the great water I spared Akut's life when I might have taken it and become king of the tribe of Akut. Now I have saved Akut from death beneath the rending fangs of Sheeta.

"When Akut or the tribe of Akut is in danger, let them call to Tarzan like this." The ape-man gave the awful cry used by the tribe of Kerchak to gather its members when danger threatened.

"And," he continued, "when they hear Tarzan call to them, let them remember what he has done for Akut and come to him with great speed. Shall it be as Tarzan says?"

"Huh!" agreed Akut, and from the rest there rose a unanimous "Huh."

Then they resumed feeding again as though nothing had happened, and with them fed John Clayton, Lord Greystoke.

He noticed, however, that Akut kept always close to him, often looking at him with a strange wonder in his little bloodshot eyes. Once he did something that Tarzan had never before seen an ape do—he found a particularly tender grub and handed it to Tarzan.

As the tribe hunted, the glistening body of the ape-man mingled with the brown, shaggy hides of his companions. Often, they brushed together in passing, but the apes had already taken his presence for granted, and he was treated just like any other ape. He felt very much at home, moving out of the way of angry she-apes with children and returning growl for growl with the belligerent young bulls. Soon it was as though he had never been among humans.

For most of a week he roamed the jungle with his new friends, partly for companionship but also to impress himself firmly on their rather short memories. It might someday be very valuable to have a tribe of great apes at his call.

When he figured that they would likely remember him, he decided to continue exploring on his own. He set out northward along the shore one day, traveling rapidly until nightfall. When the sun rose the next morning he saw that it lay almost directly to his right as he stood upon the beach, instead of straight out across the water as before. The shoreline had obviously inclined westward, so he kept moving for a second day at high speed through the trees near the shore. A worry began to grow in his mind.

When the sun set that night straight out across the water opposite the land, the ape-man realized that his worry was reality. Rokoff had marooned him on an island.

He might have known it! The Russian had left him in the worst possible position. Doubtless Rokoff had then sailed directly to the mainland, where it would be a simple matter to deliver the infant Jack to his foster parents. Tarzan shuddered. He had enough experience with African tribes to know that even though the people were generous and kind, their lives were filled with hardship and danger. And when the boy grew to manhood, he would hardly be able to function in England, if he ever got there. He pictured his son with filed teeth, a slit nose, and a painted face, and wished only for Rokoff's throat in his fingers.

And Jane!

She must be suffering terrible tortures of doubt and fear. He felt that her situation was much worse than his, for he at least knew that one of his loved ones was safe at home, while she had no idea of the whereabouts of either her husband or her son.

Luckily Tarzan did not guess the truth, for it would have made him far more miserable.

As he moved slowly through the jungle with these gloomy thoughts, he heard a strange scratching sound which he could not interpret. Cautiously he moved toward it, and presently he came upon a huge panther pinned beneath a fallen tree.

As Tarzan approached, the beast turned snarling toward him, struggling to extricate itself;

but one great branch and the smaller entangling branches held it fast.

The ape-man put an arrow in his bow to kill the helpless cat, rather than let it die of starvation. But as he drew back the shaft, a sudden whim kept him from releasing it.

Why kill the poor creature, when it would be so easy to save it? From Sheeta's futile struggles, he could see that the panther was not seriously hurt; it had no broken limbs.

Relaxing his bowstring, he re-quivered the arrow and slung his bow over his shoulder. Then he stepped closer to the pinioned beast, making the soothing, purring sound that the great cats themselves make when contented and happy. It was the friendliest approach that Tarzan could think of to offer Sheeta.

The panther ceased snarling and eyed the ape-man closely. To lift the tree's great weight from the animal it was necessary to come within reach of those long, strong talons, and afterward the man would be totally at the mercy of the savage beast; but Tarzan of the Apes knew no fear. He made up his mind.

He stepped confidently into the tangle of branches close to the panther's side, still voicing his friendly purr. The cat turned to look at the man, eyeing him steadily—questioningly. The long fangs were bared, but more in readiness than threat.

Tarzan put his broad shoulder beneath the treetrunk, and as he did so his bare leg pressed against the cat's silken side. Slowly Tarzan extended his giant muscles. The huge tree with its entangling branches rose gradually from the panther. When the great cat felt the weight lifted, it quickly crawled out from beneath. Tarzan let the tree fall back to earth, and the two beasts turned to look upon one another.

The ape-man smiled grimly, for he knew the risk. It would not have surprised him if the cat instantly sprung at him.

But it did not. Instead, Sheeta stood a few paces from the tree, watching the ape-man clamber out of the maze of fallen branches.

Now free, Tarzan was less than three paces from the panther. He might have climbed to the higher branches of the trees on the opposite side, where Sheeta could not reach him. Instead, something prompted him to approach the panther, as though searching for signs of gratitude or friendliness.

As he approached the mighty cat, the creature stepped warily to one side, and the ape-man brushed past him, within a foot of the deadly jaws. When he continued on through the forest, the panther followed him, much as a hound does. Tarzan could not tell whether the beast was following him out of friendship, or simply stalking him until it got hungry. Finally, something happened to convince him it was friendship of a sort.

Later in the day, the scent of a deer sent Tarzan into the trees. When the animal appeared beneath him, he tossed his noose around the deer's neck. Then he dropped to the ground and plunged his knife into the animal's side. Next, he called to Sheeta, using the same purr as before but a bit louder and more shrill. It was the same sound he had heard panthers use after a kill when hunting in pairs.

Almost immediately there was a crashing in the underbrush close at hand, and the long, lithe body of his strange companion broke into view.

At the sight of the body of Bara and the smell of blood, the panther gave a shrill scream. A moment later two beasts were feeding side by side upon the tender venison.

For several days this strange pair roamed the jungle together. One would make a kill and call the other. They ate well.

On one occasion they were dining on a boar that Sheeta had killed when Numa, the lion, broke through the tangled grasses close beside them. With a roar he sprang forward to steal their kill.

Sheeta bounded into a nearby thicket, while Tarzan took to the low branches of an overhanging tree and unslung his grass rope. As Numa stood above the body of the boar, head up in challenge, the ape-man dropped the noose around the maned neck and drew it tight with a sudden jerk. At the same time he called shrilly to Sheeta, and drew the struggling lion upward until only his hind feet touched the ground.

Quickly he tied the rope to a stout branch. In answer to his call, the panther leaped into sight as Tarzan dropped to earth beside the struggling and infuriated Numa. He sprang upon the lion's left side and began to stab it, while Sheeta attacked the right with tooth and claw. Before the king of beasts could slash through the rope, he hung dead in the noose.

And then the jungle air was rent by two savage cries in unison: the victory cry of the bull-ape and the panther, blended into one frightful scream.

As the last notes died away in a long-drawn, fearsome wail, twenty painted warriors were drawing their long war canoe onto the beach. They halted to stare in the direction of the jungle—and to listen.

5

Mugambi

By the time Tarzan had thoroughly explored the island, he was sure that he was the only human being there. He was getting bored, and his thoughts were gloomy. Then he had an idea. He was friends with Sheeta, as well as Akut's apes. What if he could reconcile these born enemies?

The day following the killing of Numa, Tarzan and Sheeta came upon the tribe of Akut. At sight of the panther, the great apes ran away in fear, but after a time Tarzan succeeded in recalling them. It wasn't hard to communicate his plan to the apes, though it strained their ability to understand. Getting it across to Sheeta's wicked little brain was much harder.

Among his other weapons, Tarzan had a long stout staff. He fastened his rope around the panther's neck, and got the apes to come closer. Sheeta snarled and tried to reach them but hit the end of the rope. Each time the panther did this, Tarzan hit it lightly with the staff—really more of a rebuke than a blow. Eventually the great cat came to realize that it must not attack the shaggy manlike creatures.

But why did Sheeta not turn upon Tarzan and tear him limb from limb? Twice the panther turned to growl at him, and both times it got a sharp rap on its sensitive nose. This gave the beast a healthy respect for the weapon. Sheeta was also influenced by the past few days of well-fed partnership with the ape-man. Human intelligence has a powerful influence over that of animals. That is why Tarzan could dominate so many jungle beasts who were more powerful than he.

For days the man, the panther, and the great apes roamed side by side, making and sharing their kills together. The most terrible of the group was the smooth-skinned, powerful beast who, not long before, had been a familiar figure in fashionable London homes.

Sometimes the beasts would go their own ways for an hour or a day. On one such occasion, when the ape-man had gone to sunbathe on the beach, a pair of keen eyes discovered him from the top of a nearby ridge.

Their owner looked in momentary astonishment at the figure of the odd white man basking in the tropical sun. Then he turned and made a sign to someone behind him. Presently another pair of eyes were looking down at the ape-man, and then another and another, until a full twenty African warriors were lying upon their bellies along the crest of the ridge watching the white-skinned stranger.

They were downwind from Tarzan and behind him, so he neither saw nor scented them as they began a cautious advance through the tall grass toward the sandy beach. They were big and muscular, with colorful feathery headdresses and frightfully painted faces. They looked fierce and wild.

At the foot of the ridge, they rose cautiously into crouches and advanced silently toward their unaware quarry. Their strong hands held heavy war clubs menacingly at the ready. Tarzan's sorrowful thoughts had the effect of numbing his normally keen alertness, so the tribesmen were nearly upon him before he noticed them.

His mind and muscles were still jungle-conditioned, however, and he was on his feet and facing his enemies the instant he noticed them. As he rose, the warriors leaped toward him with raised clubs and savage yells, but the foremost fell dead from a blow of the stout staff. Then the lithe, sinewy figure was among them, striking right and left with a fury, power, and precision that soon caused the remaining tribesmen to retreat.

At a short distance, they regrouped to plan new tactics. Tarzan stood watching them with arms folded and a half-smile on his handsome face. Presently they advanced on him again, this time with their heavy war spears at the ready. They were between him and the jungle, fanned out in a constantly shrinking semicircle. Tarzan could not escape the final charge, in which all the great spears would be hurled at him at once. The only escape routes were the open sea or through their ranks.

Then he had an idea that turned his smile to a broad grin. The warriors were still at a distance, slowly advancing in a fantastic war dance punctuated by savage yells and leaps, in the tradition of their tribe—the Wagambi.

Then the ape-man lifted his voice in a series of weird screams that brought the Africans to a sudden, perplexed halt. They could not believe that a human throat could have formed those beastly notes. They hesitated for a moment, then resumed their deadly advance. As they did so, a sudden crashing in the jungle behind them made them halt once more, and as they turned to look in that direction, they saw something that might well have frozen the blood of braver men than the Wagambi.

Leaping from the tangled vegetation of the jungle came a huge panther, with blazing eyes and bared fangs. Behind him was a troop of mighty, shaggy apes lumbering rapidly toward them on their short, bowed legs. Their long arms reached to the ground, where their huge knuckles bore the weight of their ponderous bodies as they lurched forward.

The beasts of Tarzan had come in answer to his call.

Before the Wagambi could recover from their astonishment, the frightful horde was upon them from one side and Tarzan of the Apes from the other. Heavy spears were hurled and mighty war clubs wielded, and though apes went down never to rise, so, too, fell the men of Ugambi.

Sheeta's cruel fangs and tearing talons ripped and tore at their dark flesh. Akut's mighty yellow tusks found the jugular of more than one mighty warrior, and Tarzan of the Apes was here and there and everywhere, urging on his fierce allies and taking a heavy toll with his long, slim knife.

In a moment the tribesmen had scattered for their lives, but of the twenty that had crept down the grassy slope only a single warrior managed to escape the horde that had overwhelmed his people. He was Mugambi, chief of the Wagambi of

Ugambi, and as he disappeared in the tangled growth on the ridge, only the keen eyes of the ape-man saw where he went.

Leaving his pack to feast on the flesh of their victims—flesh that he could not touch—Tarzan of the Apes pursued the single survivor of the bloody fray. Just beyond the ridge he came within sight of the fleeing warrior, leaping headlong for a long war canoe on the beach above the high tide line. Silently the ape-man raced after him, for the war canoe had given him a new thought. If these men had come to his island by boat, there would be other people where they came from, and even if it too was an island, it probably had contact with the African mainland.

A heavy hand fell upon Mugambi's shoulder before he was aware that he was being pursued. As he turned to do battle, giant fingers closed about his wrists and he was hurled to earth with a giant on top of him before he could strike a blow in his own defense.

In the West African dialect, Tarzan spoke to the man beneath him.

"Who are you?" he asked.

"Mugambi, chief of the Wagambi," replied the black warrior.

"I will spare your life," Tarzan said, "if you will promise to help me to leave this island. What do you answer?"

"I will help you," replied Mugambi. "But now

that you have killed all my warriors, I do not know that even I can leave your country. There is no one to paddle the canoe. Without paddlers we cannot cross the water."

Tarzan rose and let his prisoner get up. The fellow was a magnificent example of manhood—a black counterpart to the splendid white man whom he faced.

"Come!" said the ape-man, and started back in the direction of the snarling and growling of the feasting pack. Mugambi drew back.

"They will kill us," he said.

"They will not," replied Tarzan. "They are mine."

Mugambi hesitated, but Tarzan forced him to accompany him, and presently the two returned to the grisly spectacle on the beach. At sight of them the beasts looked up with menacing growls, but Tarzan strode in among them, dragging the nervous survivor with him.

It was easy to teach the apes to accept Mugambi, but as before, Sheeta was another story. The panther could not understand why it was all right to devour Mugambi's warriors, but not Mugambi. By now, however, he was full, so he was content to circle the African warrior with low, menacing growls. For his part, Mugambi thought it wise to stay close to the strange white man; none of the creatures ever threatened him.

Soon Tarzan decided to drive the lesson home

for Sheeta, so he took the great cat by the scruff of the neck and dragged it close to Mugambi. Sheeta growled at the stranger; Tarzan slapped the panther on the nose. Again it growled and was rebuked, and again and again. The sight deeply impressed Mugambi: this man was mauling one of the fiercest meat-eaters of the jungle with his bare hands. Such a thing was unheard of, and the African's respect for Tarzan grew accordingly. Soon Mugambi felt safe—if not relaxed—around Tarzan's beasts.

Before long Tarzan and Mugambi, with Sheeta and Akut, lay in wait at the watering hole as a deer approached. At a word from the ape-man, the four of them leaped out upon the terrified animal. The black warrior guessed that the poor creature died of fright before any of the hunters touched it.

Mugambi built a fire and cooked his portion of the kill, but Tarzan, Sheeta, and Akut tore theirs, raw, with their sharp teeth. This was not strange; from childhood, Mugambi had eaten only cooked meat, whereas Tarzan had not had cooked food of any sort until he was an adult and he never acquired a taste for it. Given the chance, we fall into the habits we learned as children.

Over the next few days, Tarzan tried without success to teach the apes to paddle. He did manage to get some of them to enter the frail craft, which he and Mugambi paddled about where the water was smooth. During these trips he had placed paddles in their hands, and they tried to imitate the humans, but it is hard for apes to concentrate on anything for long. It would take weeks of patient training, at the least, before the apes learned to use the paddles. In the meantime, he worked at weaving a sail of barkcloth.

Akut was the one exception. From the very first he showed an intelligent interest in this new sport. He seemed to understand the purpose of the paddles, so Tarzan took pains to explain in the ape-language how best to use them.

From Mugambi Tarzan learned that the mainland was only a short distance away. It seemed that the Wagambi warriors had ventured too far out in their frail craft, and the combination of a heavy tide and a high wind had driven them out of sight of land. After paddling for a whole night, thinking that they were headed for home, they had seen this land at sunrise. They had not learned that it was an island until Tarzan told Mugambi so.

The Wagambi chief was quite doubtful about the sail, for he had never seen one used. His country lay on a tributary the broad Ugambi River, and this was the first time any of his people had been to the ocean. Tarzan, however, was confident that with a good wind from the west he could navigate the little craft to the mainland. At any rate, it was better to die on the way than to remain forever on this island.

When the first fair wind rose, he set out on his cruise. With Tarzan rode as strange and fearsome a crew as ever sailed, for Mugambi and Akut went with him, and Sheeta, the panther, and a dozen great males of the tribe of Akut.

6

A Fearsome Crew

The war canoe headed toward the open sea. Tarzan, Mugambi, and Akut had to paddle until they were far enough out to sea for the sail to work.

Tarzan kept Sheeta in the bow near him, for the panther was hardest of the strange crew to control. In the stern was Mugambi, and just in front of him squatted Akut. Between Akut and Tarzan sat the twelve hairy apes, blinking in confusion, and now and then turning their eyes longingly back toward shore.

All went well until the canoe hit heavy seas. The tossing of the boat caused the apes to fidget and whine. Akut was able to keep them under control until a very large wave struck the canoe at the same time as a wind-squall. Then their terror took over, and they nearly overturned the boat before Akut and Tarzan could quiet them. Eventually they got used to the strange movements, and stopped causing trouble.

Other than that, the trip was uneventful. After ten hours of sailing, the shadows of the coast loomed ahead. By this time, it was too dark to determine where they were, so Tarzan ran the boat through the surf toward the shore to wait for daylight. He hoped they were near the mouth of the Ugambi.

The dugout swung broadside the instant its nose hit the sand, and Akut's apes and Sheeta scrambled madly for shore. This turned the little boat over, dumping Mugambi headfirst into the water. Shortly after, another heavy breaker hit them all from behind, pitching all of the apes face-first again into the water and flattening Mugambi as he tried to stand up. Sheeta scrambled, spat, snarled, and flailed, fortunately harming no one.

Tarzan could not keep from laughing, and his guffaws pealed through the early morning darkness. When Mugambi got to his feet in the thigh-deep salt water, spitting out the sand stirred up by the mad stampede, he in turn could not hold back his laughter. Dark eyes met blue ones across the water, and they laughed together—hard.

The surf washed the capsized canoe ashore behind them, and they all settled in to await the dawn. The soaked apes huddled close together for warmth; Mugambi quickly built a driftwood fire. Tarzan and Sheeta, however, had other ideas. Neither of them feared the jungle night, and they were hungry.

It was Tarzan who first caught the scent: a bull buffalo. Presently the two found the beast, sleeping by a river.

Closer they crept, Sheeta from one side and Tarzan from the other. They had hunted together long enough to develop teamwork. For a moment they paused, and then, at the ape-man's signal, Sheeta sprang upon the great back, burying strong teeth in the bull's neck. Instantly the brute sprang to his feet with a bellow of pain and rage. Tarzan, knife in hand, rushed in on the animal's left side, stabbing it repeatedly behind the great shoulder.

The bellowing bull raced madly off, dragging Tarzan and Sheeta through the brush. Sheeta clung stubbornly to the back, biting deep toward the spine. Several hundred yards of flight later, Tarzan's blade found the buffalo's heart. With a final agonized bellow, he plunged headlong to the earth.

Tarzan and Sheeta feasted. Afterward, they curled up together in a thicket, the man's head resting on the side of the sleeping panther. Shortly after dawn they awoke and ate again, then returned to the beach. Tarzan led the rest of the pack to the kill.

When the meal was done the animals curled up to sleep, so Tarzan and Mugambi set off in search of the Ugambi River. Barely a hundred yards away they came upon a broad stream, which the African instantly recognized as the one his warriors had paddled down to the sea. The two followed the stream down to the ocean, finding that it emptied into a bay near where they had beached the canoe.

Tarzan was delighted, for he knew that many natives lived near the rivers of the African jungle. Natives might have news of Rokoff, and, perhaps, even the baby. Mugambi told the ape-man that there was an especially ruthless native tribe upriver from his people. That sounded like the sort of place Rokoff would leave poor little Jack.

He and Mugambi hiked to the spot they had landed the night before. There, they righted and launched the dugout canoe. The pounding surf made the work difficult, but soon they were paddling up the coast toward the mouth of the Ugambi. It was hard work going against the current and tide, but Mugambi guided the boat to eddies near shore where they could make progress.

Near dusk, the African advised Tarzan that they were near the spot where they had left their traveling companions. Tying the dugout to a tree, the two made their way into the jungle. Soon they came to some of the apes eating fruit near the buffalo carcass. Sheeta was gone and did not return that night. Tarzan supposed that it had wandered off to find its own kind.

Early the next morning the ape-man led the group down to the river. As he walked, he uttered a series of shrill cries. There was a faint answering scream. A half-hour later, as the apes were gingerly boarding the canoe, Sheeta bound into view. The great beast purred like a house cat as he rubbed his sides against the ape-man. Then, at a word from Tarzan, Sheeta sprang lightly into the bow of the dugout.

Once they were all in the boat, Tarzan noticed that two of the apes were missing. Akut and he called to them for some time. Finally, getting no response, they left without them. These two had been least eager to sail from the island to begin with and had been the most terrified during the voyage. It was likely they had deserted to avoid sailing again. The strange group paddled till just after noon, then stopped to hunt.

They did not notice the slender tribesman who watched them briefly from the bushes. After a moment, he disappeared into the dense jungle.

Like a deer, this tribesman raced along the narrow trail that led to a native village several miles up the river. In his excitement, he exaggerated a bit to his chief: "Another white man is coming, with many warriors! They come in a great war canoe to kill and rob, as did the one with the hairy face!"

The chief, Kaviri, leaped to his feet. His experience of the bearded white man was both recent and bitter, filling his heart with hate. In another moment the rumble of the war drums rose from the village, calling in the hunters from the forest and the farmers from the fields.

Within minutes, seven war canoes were manned

and launched by painted warriors bearing long spears. These battleships slid noiselessly over the water, propelled by powerful muscles rolling beneath deep ebony flesh.

There was no beating of drums now, for Kaviri was a crafty general who would take no pointless chances. He planned to swoop quietly down with his seven boats on the single canoe of the white men. He could overwhelm them in close combat before their guns could do much damage.

Kaviri's own canoe was in the lead. As it rounded a sharp bend in the river, his target came suddenly into sight. At that moment, the swift current caught his dugout and swept it quickly against the boat of his enemy. The chief had just time to notice the white face in the bow of the oncoming craft before the two touched. His men sprang to their feet, yelling like mad devils and thrusting their long spears at those in the other canoe.

A moment later, when Kaviri realized what he was facing, he would have given all his wealth to be safely back in his village. Scarcely had the two boats collided than the frightful apes of Akut rose growling and barking from the bottom of the canoe. The attackers were surprised and terrified, but had no choice except to stand and fight. Now the other war canoes bore rapidly down on the two craft. Their occupants were eager to join the battle, which they thought would be against white men and their native porters.

They swarmed about Tarzan's canoe, but when they saw the situation, all but one turned and paddled swiftly upriver. That one came too close to the ape-man's craft before its occupants got a good look at the opposition. As the second canoe touched, Tarzan spoke a few low words to Sheeta and Akut.

Before the arriving canoe could retreat, there was a blood-freezing scream as a huge panther jumped into one end of their craft, and into the other end clambered a great ape. The panther slashed and cut with talon and fang, while Akut buried his yellow canines in the necks of those that came near, hurling the proud warriors overboard as he fought toward the center of the canoe.

Chief Kaviri was so busy battling with his own set of demons that he could not help his warriors in the other boat. A giant white devil had taken his spear from him as though he, the mighty Kaviri, were a child. Hairy monsters were overcoming his fighting men, and weirdest of all, a black chieftain like himself was fighting shoulder to shoulder with Kaviri's hideous enemies. Kaviri fought bravely, for he expected to die, and hoped to take an enemy down with him. To his dismay, he was no match for the strength and agility of the creature that finally found his throat and forced him into the bottom of the canoe.

Kaviri's head began to whirl. His vision dimmed, and there was a great pain in his chest as he struggled for breath. Then he blacked out.

When he opened his eyes, he was surprised to be alive, securely bound in the bottom of his own canoe. A great panther sat watching him.

Kaviri shuddered and closed his eyes again, waiting for the ferocious creature to end his life. He waited. But no fangs tore his flesh. He reopened his eyes. Beyond the panther, the white giant was paddling, and directly behind him Kaviri saw some of his own warriors doing likewise. Behind them squatted several hairy apes. Tarzan spoke as he paddled.

"Your warriors tell me that you are Kaviri, the chief of a large tribe," he said.

"Yes," replied the African.

"Why did you attack me? I came in peace."

"Another white man 'came in peace' three moons ago," Kaviri replied, "and after we had brought him presents of a goat and cassava and milk, he attacked us with his guns and killed many of my people. Then he left, taking all of our goats and many of our young men and women."

"I am not like him," replied Tarzan. "I harmed you only because you tried to harm me. Tell me, what was the face of this bad white man like? I am searching for one who has wronged me, and this may be him."

"He was a very wicked-looking man with a bad face, covered with a great, black beard."

"Was there a little white child with him?"

asked Tarzan, his heart pounding.

"No," replied Kaviri, "the white child was with the other group."

"Other group!" exclaimed Tarzan. "What other group?"

"With the group that the very bad white man was chasing. There was a white man, woman, and the child, with six Mosula porters. They passed up the river three days ahead of the very bad white man."

A white man, woman, and child! The child must be his little Jack; but who could the woman be—and the man? Was it possible that one of Rokoff's thugs had conspired with some woman to steal the baby from him? If so, they were probably going to take the child back to civilization for a reward—or for ransom.

But now that Rokoff had chased them far upriver, he would eventually overtake them—unless they were captured and killed by the fierce natives further up the Ugambi. Tarzan was now convinced that Rokoff intended to deliver the baby to that dangerous tribe upstream.

As he talked to Kaviri, the canoes had been moving steadily upriver toward the chief's village. Kaviri's warriors paddled, casting nervous glances at their strange passengers. Three of Akut's apes had been killed in the battle, but Akut and seven others survived, as had Sheeta. The men's nerves were not helped by the constant growling and snarling of the animals; in fact, it was all Tarzan and Akut and Mugambi could do to control them. The men rowed for all they were worth.

At Kaviri's camp Tarzan paused only long enough to eat the food that the tribe offered him, and arrange with the chief for a dozen men to paddle his canoe. Kaviri was glad to do whatever could hurry the horrid pack on its way. Unfortunately, it was not easy to convince any of the villagers to go with Tarzan and his unusual crew; when Kaviri's people learned the plan, the entire tribe fled into the jungle.

Tarzan could not help smiling. "They do not seem anxious to come," he said; "but just remain quietly here, Kaviri, and presently your people will flock to you."

Then the ape-man rose and called his pack to him. Leaving Mugambi to keep an eye on Kaviri, he disappeared in the jungle with Sheeta and the apes at his heels.

For half an hour the silence was broken only by the ordinary sounds of jungle life. Kaviri and Mugambi sat waiting in the empty village.

Presently from a great distance came a hideous sound. Mugambi recognized the weird challenge of the ape-man. Immediately, from different parts of the jungle, rose a horrid semicircle of similar shrieks and screams, punctuated now and again by the blood-curdling cry of a hungry panther.

7

Betrayed

Kaviri and Mugambi squatted before the entrance to Kaviri's hut. Kaviri's face revealed his alarm.

"What is that awful noise?" he whispered.

"It is Tarzan and his people," replied Mugambi. "But I do not know what they are doing, unless they are devouring your people."

Kaviri shuddered and looked fearfully toward the jungle. In all his long life, he had never heard such a frightening uproar.

Closer and closer came the sounds, mingled with the terrified shrieks of men, women, and children. For twenty long minutes the blood-curdling cries continued, growing ever closer. Kaviri rose to flee, but Mugambi seized and held him, as Tarzan had ordered.

A moment later a horde of terrified natives burst from the jungle, racing toward the shelter of their huts. Behind them came Tarzan and Sheeta and the apes of Akut, driving the villagers like frightened sheep.

Presently Tarzan stood before Kaviri, the old quiet smile on his lips.

"Your people have returned, my brother," he said, "and now you may select those who are to paddle my canoe."

Kaviri got shakily to his feet, calling his people out of their huts. None came.

"Tell them," suggested Tarzan, "that I will send my people in after them."

Kaviri did so, and soon the entire population came forth, their frightened eyes glued to the savage creatures that wandered about the village.

Quickly Kaviri chose a dozen warriors to accompany Tarzan. The poor fellows were terrified at the idea of traveling with the panther and the apes, but Kaviri explained to them that Tarzan's beasts would chase them if they attempted to evade the duty. Finally they went gloomily down to the river and took their places in the canoe. Their chieftain sighed in relief when the unwanted visitors finally disappeared around a river-bend.

For three days the strange company continued deeper into the wild country along the Ugambi. Three of Kaviri's paddlers deserted; but several of the apes had finally mastered the paddles, so Tarzan did not try to bring the deserters back. He could have traveled faster on land, but the boat tended to keep his wild crew together. Twice a day they landed to hunt and feed, and at night they slept on the riverbank.

There were villages, but the inhabitants fled in alarm at the sight of this fearsome crew, leaving only deserted huts. Tarzan was anxious to speak with the people, but this seemed unlikely while he traveled this way. He decided to go by land and have the others follow him by boat. He explained this to Mugambi, and ordered Akut to obey the African's directions.

"I will join you again in a few days," he said. "I am going ahead to learn what has become of the very bad white man I am looking for."

At the next halt Tarzan took to the shore and was soon lost to their view.

The first few villages he came to were deserted, evidence of the speed with which news of his pack had traveled. But toward evening, he came to a distant cluster of thatched huts surrounded by a fence of pointed stakes, inhabited by a couple of hundred natives.

The women were making dinner as Tarzan of the Apes took a position above them in a giant tree overhanging the fence around the village. How could he make contact without either terrifying or provoking them? The last thing he wanted was to fight every tribe he met. At last he came up with a plan.

After making sure he was well hidden in the tree, he gave a few hoarse Sheeta-like grunts. All eyes immediately turned in his direction, straining to see the intruder in the dusk. When he had their attention, he gave the shrill scream of the panther. Then, without stirring a leaf, he crept to the ground outside the fence and ran to the village gate. Pounding on it, he shouted: he was a friend asking food and shelter for the night.

Tarzan had known many native villages. The grunting and screaming of Sheeta in the tree above them would set their nerves on edge, and his pounding on the gate after dark would make it worse. He was not surprised that he got no reply, because natives tend to be suspicious of voices in the night; many believe that ghosts and demons lurk there. He called out again.

"Let me in, my friends!" he cried. "I am a white man, pursuing the wicked white man who passed this way a few days ago. I will punish him for his crimes against you and me. To prove my friendship, I will drive Sheeta back into the jungle—away from you. But if you do not promise to welcome me, I will let Sheeta stay and devour you."

For a moment there was silence. Then an elderly voice replied:

"If you are indeed a friend, we will let you in—but first you must drive Sheeta away."

"Very well," Tarzan said. "Listen, and you will hear Sheeta fleeing."

The ape-man returned quickly to the tree, and this time he made a lot of climbing and growling sounds, panther-style. When he was high in the branches that hung over the fence, he began a great commotion, shaking the tree violently. He ordered the imaginary panther to flee or perish, and threw in a few screams and snarls of anger. Presently he swung to the opposite side of the tree and off into the jungle, pounding loudly against the treetrunks, making the panther's growls seem to be fading into the distance.

A few minutes later he returned to the village gate.

"I have driven Sheeta away," he called out. "Now keep your promise and let me in."

After some excited discussion, six warriors came to open the gates, peering out warily to see what was outside. The weird sight of a nearly-naked white man did not reassure them much. Tarzan reaffirmed his friendly intent in quiet tones, in their own language, and soon they opened the gate just enough to let him in.

As he walked through the village toward the chief's hut, he was surrounded by many curious onlookers. The chief told him that Rokoff had passed upriver a week ago, and that he had horns growing from his forehead, and was accompanied by a thousand devils. The chief said that the evil white man had stayed here a month. While none of these statements quite agreed with Kaviri's, Tarzan could find only slight fault with the description of Rokoff and his henchmen. Mainly, it confirmed that he was on the right trail—and that it led inland.

In the interior of Africa, Rokoff could never escape Tarzan of the Apes.

After several hours of questioning, the ape-man learned that another group had preceded the Russian by several days. There had been three whites—a man, a woman, and a little man-child—and several Mosulas.

Tarzan explained that his people would be along in a canoe, probably the next day. He would continue on, but if the chief would give Mugambi and those with him a friendly reception, they would do no harm to the chief's people. "And now," he concluded, "I am going to get some sleep. Let no one disturb me."

The chief offered him a hut, but Tarzan preferred the open air under the tree. He also had a plan. He gave the excuse of wanting to be ready should Sheeta return, to which the leader was quite agreeable.

Mighty though he was, Tarzan was only one man in Africa, always greatly outnumbered by natives. For this reason, he had always felt it wise to leave them with the impression that he possessed miraculous powers. And so, when the village was quiet in sleep, he arose and leaped into the branches of the tree to fade silently into the black mystery of the jungle night.

For the rest of the night the ape-man swung rapidly through the upper and middle terraces of the forest, his way lighted by the moon. At dawn he stopped to feed and take a nap. He awoke toward noon and continued in pursuit of his enemy.

Twice he came upon villages. The situations were delicate, but he succeeded in each instance in quieting their fears and in heading off potentially hostile intentions toward him. From them he learned that he was still on the Russian's trail.

Two more days up the Ugambi, he came to a large village. The chief, a fierce-looking fellow with sharp-filed teeth, seemed friendly. The ape-man was now in need of a good night's sleep. He wanted to be fresh and strong when he caught up with Rokoff, which must happen soon.

The chief told him that the bearded white man had just left the morning before. He claimed to know nothing of the other group with the little child. Tarzan did not like the chief's appearance or manner; he spoke pleasantly, but also seemed to have a certain contempt for this half-naked white man who came without followers or presents to offer. Even so, the ape-man needed food and rest, and he knew no fear of man, beast, or devil. And so he curled up in the shadow of a hut and went to sleep.

Scarcely had he dozed off when the chief called two of his swiftest warriors and whispered quick instructions to them; a moment later they were racing upstream. Meanwhile, the chief kept the village quiet. No one was allowed to approach the sleeping visitor or make any noise that might disturb him.

Three hours later several canoes came silently into view from upriver propelled rapidly by the sure strokes and brawny muscles of experienced African crews. The chief stood on the bank, his spear held horizontally overhead in a pre-arranged signal: it meant that the white stranger was still sleeping peacefully.

In the bows of two of the canoes were the chief's runners. Their mission had been to catch up with this group and bring them back. In a few moments the dugouts were ashore. The native warriors got out, accompanied by a half-dozen sullen, ugly-looking white men. None looked more evil than the black-bearded man in command.

"Where is the white man your messengers spoke of?" he asked the chief.

"This way," replied the chief. "I have made sure no one awakened him. I do not know that he means you harm, but he questioned me closely about you and your movements, and he looks like the one you described—the one you thought was safe in the place you call Jungle Island.

"If I had not recognized him, he might have hunted and slain you. If he in fact is your enemy, I should like very much to have a rifle and some ammunition as a reward for helping you," finished the chief meaningfully.

"You have done well," replied the white man, "and you shall have your reward, as long as you stand with me."

"I shall," said the chief. "And now come and see this stranger who sleeps within my village." He led the way to the hut near which Tarzan slept peacefully. Behind them came the remaining whites and twenty warriors, gestured to complete silence by the chief and his bearded accomplice.

As they turned the corner of the hut on tiptoe, an ugly smile touched the lips of the bearded man as he saw the sleeping ape-man's giant figure. Then he turned to those behind him, pointed to the sleeping man, and motioned for them to seize him and tie him up.

A moment later, a surprised Tarzan found himself subdued and securely bound by a dozen men before he could make an effort to escape. Then they rolled him face-up, and as his eyes turned toward the crowd, they fell on the sneering face of Nikolai Rokoff. He stepped quite close to Tarzan.

"Pig!" he cried. "Have you not learned to keep away from Nikolai Rokoff?"

Then he kicked the helpless man full in the face.

"That is your welcome," he said. "Tonight, before my friends torture you to death, I shall tell you what has already happened to your wife and child, and of my further plans for them."

8

The Dance of Death

Through the luxuriant vegetation of the jungle night, a great sleek body traveled in utter silence upon its soft padded feet. Only two blazing points of yellow-green flame shone occasionally in the moonlight. From time to time the beast would stop to sniff searchingly, or to dart momentarily up into the branches. It scented many a tender four-footed creature, and its cruel mouth watered, but it strangely ignored the appetite that normally would have sent the rolling, fur-clad muscles flying at some soft throat. It traveled all that night, halting the next day only to make a single kill, which it tore to fragments and devoured with sullen rumbles as though half-starved.

By dusk it was approaching the tall stake fence of a large native village. A shadow of swift and silent death, it circled the village with nose to ground. At last it halted in a spot where several huts nearly touched the wall; it sniffed, then turned its head to one side to listen.

No human ear could have detected what it

heard, but the creature was immediately trans-
formed. As if propelled by steel springs, it leaped
quickly and silently to the top of the fence, then
down again to disappear stealthily into the dark
space between the wall and the back of a hut.

In the center of the village, women were hard
at work preparing a great feast for the evening.
Close to a stout stake near the cooking-fires, a little group of African warriors stood talking. Their
faces and bodies were painted in white, blue, and

orange; their hair was decorated with clay and bright parrot feathers.

Meanwhile, in a hut to one side, the 'entertainment' awaited. Tarzan of the Apes strained at his bonds with mighty muscles, but the Russian knew his work. Not even the ape-man's giant brawn could budge them.

Death!

Tarzan had looked the Grim Hunter in the face many times, and smiled. And he would smile again tonight when he knew the end was near; but now he thought only of his loved ones.

Jane would never know how it happened. He thanked heaven for that, and that she at least was safe in London, among kind and loving friends who would comfort her.

But the boy!

Tarzan writhed at the thought of him. His son! And now he—the mighty Lord of the Jungle, the only one in the world able to save the child from Rokoff's evil plans—had been trapped like a slow-witted ox. He would die in a few hours and with him the child's last chance of being rescued.

Knowing that Tarzan was safely tied up, Rokoff had been in to insult and abuse him several times during the afternoon. To the Russian's disgust, his giant captive had not uttered a sound. Rokoff had decided to save the worst torture for the last moment before the African spears put an end to his hated enemy forever: he would reveal the true location of Jane. He found great satisfaction in the thought that, in Tarzan's dying moments, the ape-man would learn that his wife was not safe in England.

The dusk was darkening, and the ape-man could hear the preparations going forward for the torture and the feast. There would be a dance of death, of the sort he had seen before; this time he was the victim. The warriors would circle him with spears, showing off their great skill by cutting and stabbing so that he did not pass out or die. Tarzan was not afraid, for he had seen much blood and cruel death, nor would he give up hope until the final moment. If they grew careless for even an instant, his cunning mind and giant muscles would gain him escape—and revenge.

As he lay thinking about his fate, he suddenly noticed a faint and familiar scent. Then his sharp ears heard indications of a quiet presence just behind his hut. His lips moved, making a sound that no human ear outside would hear—for the intended listener was not human.

An instant later he heard the soft sound of a fur-clad body and padded feet scaling the outer wall behind the hut. Then came a tearing at the hut's wall, and through the hole slunk a great beast, pressing its cold muzzle close to his neck.

Sheeta, the panther.

The beast snuffed round the bound man, whining a little. There was a limit to their communication: Sheeta could surely see that he was helpless, but could the cat understand Tarzan's dangerous situation? What had brought the beast to him? Its coming was a good sign. But when the ape-man tried to get Sheeta to bite through his bonds, the great animal did not understand, and merely licked his wrists and arms.

After a few moments, the two heard the sound of someone approaching the hut. Sheeta gave a low growl and slunk into a dark corner. Evidently, the visitor did not hear the warning sound, for he walked into the hut. He was a tall, grim African warrior. He went to Tarzan's side and pricked him with a spear. The ape-man let forth a weird sound, and in answer to it, a bolt of fur-clad death leaped from the shadows to strike the painted warrior full on the chest. Sharp talons dug into his flesh, and great yellow fangs into the throat. A fearful scream of anguish mixed with the scream of the killing panther. Then all was silent, except for the rending of bloody flesh and the crunching of human bones between mighty jaws.

The noise hushed the village for a moment. Then voices spoke, some high-pitched and fearful, others the deep, low tones of authority. Tarzan and the panther heard the approaching footsteps of many men. Then, to Tarzan's surprise, the great cat rose from its kill and slunk noiselessly out the hole it had ripped. He heard the body scrape over the top of the wall, then nothing more of the panther.

From the other side, he could hear bare feet approaching to investigate.

He had little hope that Sheeta would return. If the great cat intended to defend him against all comers, it would have remained by his side. His kind were strange; they could be fearless in the face of certain death, yet at other times, timid. Likely the sound of the approaching warriors had frightened off the panther.

So? He had expected to die. What might Sheeta have done for him, other than to maul a couple of his enemies before being shot down by a rifle? Had the cat been able to release him, it would have been a different story, but Tarzan abandoned hope of rescue by that means.

The natives were at the entrance to the hut now, peering fearfully into the dark interior. Two advanced, very cautiously, bearing lighted torches and ready spears. Those behind them pushed them forward into the ominous silence of the hut.

Presently one of the unwilling scouts had a clever idea, and flung his lighted torch into the center of the hut. The interior lit up for a few seconds before the flame went out on the earth floor.

The white prisoner was still as securely bound as before. In the center of the hut another figure lay motionless, its throat and chest savagely mangled. This was far more terrifying for them than if Sheeta had been there, for they saw their fellow horribly dead with no reasonable cause. Lacking a natural explanation, they sought a supernatural one: it must have been the ghastly work of evil spirits. The scouts ran screaming from the hut, knocking over anyone in the way.

For an hour Tarzan heard only the murmur of excited voices from the far end of the village. The tribesmen sounded like they were trying to work up the courage to return to the haunted hut, for now and then came a savage yell, as if on the field of battle. But in the end it was two of the whites who first entered, carrying torches and guns. Tarzan was not surprised to discover that neither of them was Rokoff. He knew his enemy was too great a coward to risk his own skin.

When they saw that the white men were not attacked, the natives crowded into the interior, their voices hushed with terror as they looked upon the mutilated corpse of their comrade. The whites demanded an explanation from Tarzan, but he merely shook his head with a grim, knowing smile.

At last Rokoff came. His face grew very white at the sight of the bloody face grinning up at him from the floor, frozen in its final horror.

"Come!" he said to the chief. "Let us finish off this demon before he can do the same to more of your people."

The chief gave orders that Tarzan should be carried to the stake. It was several minutes before he could convince any of his men to touch the prisoner, but at last four of the younger warriors dragged Tarzan roughly from the hut. When nothing happened, they became more confident. Once outside the hut, twenty howling warriors pushed the prisoner to the center of the village. He was bound to the post in the center of the circle of little fires, where the scent of cooking deer and boar rose from boiling pots.

Only when it was clear that Tarzan was totally helpless did Rokoff find the courage to approach him. He stepped close to the ape-man and seized a spear from a warrior, so that he could be the first to prod the bound victim. A little stream of blood trickled down the giant's smooth skin from the wound in his side, but he was silent. His smile of contempt seemed to infuriate the Russian, who flew at him with a volley of oaths, punching and kicking. When he raised the heavy spear to drive it through the mighty heart, Tarzan of the Apes was still smiling scornfully at him.

Before Rokoff could drive the weapon home, the chief sprang on him and dragged him away from his intended victim.

"Stop!" he cried. "Rob us of this prisoner and our death-dance, and you may take his place."

The Russian stopped assaulting the prisoner, but continued to taunt and insult him. Rokoff smiled to himself as he thought about the fate of Tarzan's son. And he promised himself that, before he got his final revenge on Jane, he would show her the severed head of her husband.

"You think your wife is safe in England," Rokoff said. "Poor fool! At this moment she is in the hands of scum, far from the safety of London. I was going to tell you this when I returned to Jungle Island with proof of her fate. Now that you are about to die as you deserve, I will leave it to your imagination what is being done to her."

The dance began now, and the yells of the circling warriors drowned Rokoff's further taunts. The leaping warriors, the flickering firelight playing on their painted bodies, circled about the victim at the stake.

Tarzan recalled another scene like this, when he had rescued D'Arnot from a similar situation just before the final spear-thrust would have ended his friend's sufferings. Who was there now to rescue him? No one in the world could save him from torture and death.

The dancers leaped closer now. The spears flicked his body in the first torturing stabs that would lead to more serious thrusts.

The end was near. The ape-man longed for the last savage lunge that would end his misery.

And then from the depths of the jungle rose a shrill scream.

For an instant the dancers paused. In the moment of silence, the bound white man gave an answering shriek—one more fearsome than the scream of the jungle beast a moment before.

For several minutes the warriors hesitated;

then, at the urging of Rokoff and their chief, they leaped in to finish the dance and the victim. But before another spear touched the tanned flesh, a smooth streak of green-eyed hate and ferocity bounded from the door of the prison hut. Sheeta, the panther, stood snarling beside its master.

For an instant black and white alike stood motionless in terror. Their eyes were riveted on the bared fangs of the jungle cat.

Only Tarzan of the Apes saw what else was emerging from the dark interior of the hut.

9

Nobility or Villainy

From her cabin port on the *Kincaid*, Jane Clayton had seen her husband rowed ashore on Jungle Island. The ship then resumed its journey.

For several days she saw no one other than Sven Anderssen, the *Kincaid's* quiet, filthy cook. She asked him the name of the island.

"Ay tink it blow purty soon purty hard," replied the Swede, and would say no more. She concluded that he spoke no other English, and stopped asking him questions; but she always greeted him pleasantly, and thanked him for the nauseating meals he brought.

Three days after Tarzan had been marooned, the *Kincaid* dropped anchor in the mouth of a great river. Presently Rokoff came to Jane Clayton's cabin.

"We have arrived, my dear," he said, with a sickening leer. "I have come to offer you safety, liberty, and ease. My heart has been softened toward you, and I wish to make amends.

"Your husband was a brute, as you best know,

for you found him naked in the jungle, roaming wild with the savage beasts. I, however, am a gentleman—born of noble blood, and raised a man of quality.

"To you, dear Jane, I offer the love of a man of culture and refinement. You must surely have had time to realize that in your girlish haste, you thoughtlessly married a lowly ape. I love you, Jane. You have but to say the word and your suffering shall end. Your baby shall be returned to you unharmed."

Outside the door Sven Anderssen paused with the lunch he had brought. His little head was cocked to one side to eavesdrop.

As Rokoff waited for her reply, the look of surprise upon Jane Clayton's face turned to one of disgust. She shuddered.

"I would not have been surprised, Monsieur Rokoff," she said, "if you had attempted to force me to submit to your evil desires. I never imagined that you could be so stupid as to believe that I, Mrs. John Clayton, would come to you willingly, even to save my life. I have known you for a scoundrel, but I had not thought you a fool."

Rokoff's eyes narrowed and his cheeks grew red with humiliation. He took a threatening step forward.

"We shall see who is the fool," he hissed, "when I have broken you to my will and your ill-bred Yankee stubbornness has cost you all that you love—even the life of your baby—for, by the bones of St. Peter, I'll change my plans for the brat. I shall cut its heart out before your eyes. You will learn what it means to insult Nikolai Rokoff."

Jane Clayton turned wearily away.

"What is the use," she said, "of bragging about your beastly vengeance? You cannot move me either by threats or deeds. My baby cannot judge yet for himself, but I, his mother, can foresee this: if he were to live to manhood, he would willingly sacrifice his life for the honor of his mother. I will not trade my honor to save his life. If I did that, he would despise my memory to his dying day."

His failure to terrify Jane infuriated Rokoff. His claims of love were lies, of course, but his twisted mind had come up with a new idea for revenge: force her to buy her life and her child's by surrendering to his demands, then flaunt the wife of Lord Greystoke in European society as his mistress.

Again he stepped closer to her, his evil face convulsed with rage and desire. Like a wild beast he sprang at her, grasping her throat and forcing her backward onto the berth.

At the same instant the door of the cabin opened noisily. Rokoff leaped to his feet and turned to find the Swedish cook. The man's normally clever eyes were now the picture of stupidity, his lower jaw slack and foolish-looking. He busied himself in arranging Lady Greystoke's meal on the tiny table in her cabin.

The Russian glared at him.

"What do you mean," he cried, "entering here without permission? Get out!"

The cook turned his watery blue eyes toward Rokoff and smiled idiotically.

"Ay tink it blow purty soon purty hard," he said, and then he began rearranging the few dishes on the little table.

"Get out of here, or I'll throw you out, you miserable blockhead!" roared Rokoff, taking a threatening step toward the Swede.

Anderssen continued to smile foolishly in his direction, but one dirty hand slid stealthily to the handle of the long, slim knife in his soiled apron. Rokoff saw the move and stopped. Then he turned toward Jane Clayton.

"I will give you until tomorrow," he said—in French, so the cook would not understand—"to reconsider my offer. All will be sent ashore except you and the child, Paulvitch, and myself. Then you will be able to watch the baby die without interruption." With that, he banged out of the cabin without another look at the man who had interrupted his wicked business.

When he had gone, Sven Anderssen turned toward Lady Greystoke. The idiotic expression was replaced by one of cunning.

"He tink Ay ben a fool," he said. "He ben the fool. Ay savvy Franch."

Jane Clayton looked at him in surprise.

"You understood it all, then?"

Anderssen grinned. "You bet."

"And you heard what was happening and came to protect me?"

"You ben good to me," explained the Swede. "He treat me like darty dog. Ay help you, lady. You yust vait—Ay help you. Ay ben Vest Coast Africa lots times."

"But how can you help me, Sven," she asked, "against all these men?"

"Ay tink," said Sven Anderssen, "it blow purty soon purty hard," and then he turned and left the cabin.

Though Jane Clayton doubted he could do much for her, she was deeply grateful for what he already had done. To have one friend among these enemies gave her the first ray of comfort so far in this miserable, long, fearful voyage.

She saw no more of Rokoff that day. When Sven came with her dinner, she tried to ask him more about his plans, but got nothing other than his usual weather forecast. He seemed to have relapsed into stupidity. However, when he returned later to get the empty dishes, he whispered very low: "Leave on your clothes an' roll up your blankets. Ay come back after you purty soon."

He would have left at once, but Jane laid her hand upon his sleeve.

"My baby?" she asked. "I cannot go without him."

"You do vat Ay tell you," said Anderssen, scowling. "Ay ben halpin' you, so don't you gat too fonny."

When he had gone, Jane Clayton sank down upon her berth in confusion. What should she do? She began to suspect the Swede's intentions. Would she be worse off in Sven's hands than she was now? No, better to be with the devil himself than with Nikolai Rokoff. She swore a dozen times that she would not leave the *Kincaid* without her baby, and yet she remained clothed long past her usual bedtime, rolling her blankets neatly and binding them with stout cord.

About midnight there was a stealthy scratching at her door.

She crossed the room and drew the bolt. The door swung open to admit the Swede. He had a bundle of blankets under one arm. With his other grimy hand, a finger pressed to his lips commanded silence.

"Carry this," he said. "Do not make some noise vhen you see it. It ben you kid."

Quick hands snatched the bundle from the cook, and hungry mother arms clutched the sleeping infant tightly. Hot tears of joy ran down her cheeks and her whole frame shook with feeling.

"Come!" said Anderssen. "Ve got no time to vaste."

He snatched up her bundle of blankets and, outside the cabin door, his own as well. Then he led her to the ship's side and helped her down the rope ladder, holding the child for her as she climbed to the boat waiting below. A moment later he cut the rope that held the small boat to the steamer's side, and bent to the muffled oars. Soon he was rowing toward the black shadows of the Ugambi River. He seemed to know his way.

After half an hour the moon broke through the clouds to reveal a stream merging with the Ugambi. The Swede piloted the small boat up this stream. Jane Clayton wondered if the man knew where he was going. She did not know that earlier that day he had rowed up this very stream to barter with a native village, and to plan for this journey.

Even though the moon was full, the river's surface was quite dark. Giant trees overhung its narrow banks, heavy with Spanish moss and vines. Now and then they would spot a huge crocodile, startled by the splashing of the oars, or a family of hippos snorting and blowing. From the dense jungles on either side came the weird night cries of predators—the maniacal voice of the hyena, the coughing grunt of the panther, the deep roar of the lion. Jane huddled in the stern, frightened, but taking joy in the knowledge that dawn would let her look upon the baby's face.

It was close to three o'clock in the morning when Anderssen brought the boat near to shore at a clearing. From here they could dimly make out a cluster of native huts encircled by a protective barrier constructed of thorny brush.

A native woman let them through the gate. She was the wife of the chief that Anderssen had paid to help them. She took them to the chief's hut, but Anderssen said that they would sleep outside on the ground. Her duty done, the African woman left them. The Swede spread Jane's blankets out for her, then unrolled his own, and went to sleep. It was some time before Jane could get comfortable, but at last she fell asleep from utter exhaustion, clasping the baby close.

When she awoke it was broad daylight. Around her were clustered about twenty curious natives, mostly men. Instinctively, Jane Clayton drew the baby closer. But she soon saw that they did not intend to harm her or Jack. One even offered her a gourd of some kind of milk; while it was too grimy-looking for her to stomach, the spirit of the gift touched her deeply. Her face broke into one of the radiant smiles that had made her beauty famous in Baltimore and London. She raised the gourd to her lips as best she could, but the smell bothered her so much she was not sure she could get it down. Anderssen came to her rescue, taking the gourd and drinking a portion, then returning it to the giver along with a string of blue beads.

The sun was shining brightly now, and though the baby still slept, Jane could barely restrain her impatient desire to have at least a brief glance at the beloved face. The natives had withdrawn at a command from their chief, who now stood nearby talking with Anderssen.

As she debated with herself whether or not to disturb the child's sleep, she noticed that the cook spoke with the chief in his own language. What a remarkable man the fellow was! She had thought him stupid all this time; within the past twenty-four hours, she had learned that he spoke not only English and French but even the West African dialect. She had thought him shifty and untrustworthy, but so far he had proven the opposite. Still, Jane could not believe that his motives stemmed from generosity and kindheartedness. Perhaps he had hidden plans and intentions. Looking at his close-set eyes and ugly features, it was hard for her to imagine their owner having noble virtues.

Now there came a little sound from the bundle in her lap, and then a gurgling coo that made her heart leap with joy. The baby was awake! Now she might feast her eyes on him.

Quickly she snatched the blanket from the infant's face as Anderssen watched. He saw her stagger to her feet, holding the baby at arm's length from her, her eyes glued in horror on the little chubby face and twinkling eyes.

Then he heard her piteous cry as her knees gave way beneath her, and she sank to the ground and wept.

10

The Swede

As the warriors encircling Tarzan and Sheeta realized that the intruder was a flesh-and-blood panther, they took heart. In the face of all those circling spears, even the mighty Sheeta had little hope.

Rokoff was urging the chief to order his spearmen to throw. Just as the leader was about to give the order, his eyes strayed beyond Tarzan, following the gaze of the ape-man.

With a yell of terror the chief turned and fled toward the village gate. When his people and the whites looked to see what had frightened him, they too turned and ran. Lumbering down upon them, their huge forms exaggerated by the play of moonlight and campfire, came the hideous apes of Akut.

As the tribe and Rokoff's thugs turned to flee, the ape-man's savage cry rang out above the terrified shrieks. In answer, Sheeta and the apes leaped growling after the fugitives. Some of the warriors turned to give battle but went down to bloody death before the ferocious beasts of Tarzan. Others were dragged down as they fled. Only when the last of the villagers had disappeared into the jungle could Tarzan recall his savage pack to his side.

To his annoyance, he could not make even the relatively intelligent Akut—much less the others—realize that he wanted to be freed from the stake. Eventually, of course, the idea would filter through their thick skulls, but time was short. At some point the villagers would retake their home, probably assisted by the whites firing rifles from trees.

As for Sheeta, the great cat understood even less than the apes, but Tarzan marveled at its affectionate behavior. It was now walking slowly back and forth about the stake, rubbing its sides against his legs and purring like a house cat. It had surely gone to bring the rest of the pack to his rescue. His Sheeta was indeed a jewel among beasts.

Mugambi's absence, however, was worrisome. He attempted to learn from Akut what had become of the African. He feared that, without Tarzan there to restrain the animals, the beasts might have devoured Mugambi. The great ape only pointed back into the jungle.

Tarzan spent the night still tied to the stake. Shortly after dawn, his fears were realized: the villagers could be seen moving stealthily about the edge of the jungle. When full daylight came, they would be ready to evict the animals from their village. Unless some form of superstitious fear again affected the tribe, the result was certain. The animals could not stand up to overwhelming numbers of long spears and poisoned arrows for very long.

Soon the tribe's warriors began to gather at the edge of the clearing for a charge. Stealth was abandoned; they danced and leaped, shouting taunts and fierce war cries toward the village. This, Tarzan knew, was their way of building up morale for battle. Even if their first charge failed to recapture the village, the second or third would get them through the gate. It could only end in the extermination of Tarzan's bold but undisciplined defenders.

The first charge carried the howling warriors into the open. A shrill challenge from the ape-man summoned the beasts to battle, and the warriors withdrew to a safe distance after a brief skirmish.

Another half-hour of posturing and yelling followed, then they charged again. This time they nearly got to the village gate when Sheeta and the apes leaped among them, killing several and sending the rest back to the forest.

A third time the dancing and shouting was repeated; this time Tarzan was sure they would finish the job. To have come so close to rescue, only to fail because he could not teach his savage friends to release him, was most irritating. But he did not blame them. They had done their best and would now remain to die in his defense.

The Africans were preparing for the charge. A few individuals had advanced a short distance toward the village and were urging the others to follow them. In a moment the whole force would be racing across the clearing.

Tarzan thought of the little child somewhere in this cruel wilderness. His heart ached for the son that he could no longer save and for Jane's suffering. He thought of nothing else; there was no more hope.

The black warriors were halfway across the clearing when Tarzan saw an ape glaring toward one of the huts. Following the animal's gaze, he saw the mighty form of Mugambi racing toward him. He rushed to Tarzan's side. As the first villager reached the gate, the African's knife severed the last of the cords.

Throughout the village were the corpses of those killed the night before. From one of these Tarzan seized a spear and club. Then, with Mugambi at his side and the snarling pack about him, he met the natives as they poured through the gate.

Fierce and terrible was the battle that ensued, but at last the villagers were driven back. They might have overcome the small force opposing them, but the sight of two huge men—one black and one white—fighting alongside a panther and a troop of fierce apes was too much for them.

One prisoner was taken, and Tarzan promised him his liberty in return for information about Rokoff. The African told all he knew: early in the morning, their chief had tried to convince the whites to help get the village back. Rokoff had seemed far more frightened than the chief's warriors. He had been too cowardly to even approach the village again. Instead he had hurriedly taken his party down to the river, then stolen a number of the tribe's canoes. They had last been seen headed upstream, forcing the porters from Kaviri's village to paddle furiously.

So once more Tarzan of the Apes, with his African friend and his beasts, resumed the search for his son and the kidnapper. Three of Akut's apes had fallen in the fighting at the village. This left five great apes, including Akut, to accompany Sheeta, Mugambi, and Tarzan.

For weary days they traveled upriver through nearly uninhabited country, only to learn at last that they were on the wrong trail. The ape-man spoke with groups of natives along the way, but there were no longer even rumors of the white man, woman, and child. Nor could he learn any news of the Russian. He knew, however, that his best hope for finding his son was to follow his dangerous enemy.

Realizing that they must be on the wrong trail, Tarzan and his crew retraced their path back down the river. Soon he rediscovered Rokoff's trail at a point where the Russian had left the river and headed north into the brush. Tarzan concluded that the white man and woman had probably taken the child overland, away from the river, and Rokoff had followed not far behind them. Natives along the way reported having heard of or having seen Rokoff's group, but there was no news of the man and woman traveling with the child.

It was difficult to get in touch with the natives, most of whom fled into the brush at sight of Tarzan's animals; often he had to go ahead of the pack, or waylay the occasional lone warrior he caught in the jungle.

One day he came upon an unsuspecting warrior, preparing to hurl a spear. Creeping closer, the ape-man saw the target: a wounded white man crouched in a clump of bush at the trail's side. Tarzan recognized the repulsive features of the white at once: the close-set eyes, the shifty expression, the drooping yellow moustache. This man, he recalled, had not been with Rokoff's henchmen in the village where the ape-man had been a prisoner. Now he understood: this was the man fleeing from the Russian with a woman and a child, and the woman had been Jane Clayton.

The ape-man felt anger wash over him. Across his forehead stood out a broad band of scarlet, the scar marking where an enemy had long ago torn a strip of the ape-man's scalp from his skull. Tarzan looked at the pasty, weathered face of the Swede. This man had done something with his wife and child. This Swede was his rightful prey.

With that thought, he leaped on the African warrior, ruining the spear-cast. The warrior drew his knife to do battle. The Swede witnessed a duel such as he had never dreamed to see: two half-naked men, one black and one white, battling first with primitive weapons and then with hands and teeth like brutes.

For a time Anderssen did not recognize the newcomer. When he finally recognized the giant, he could hardly believe that this growling, biting beast could ever have been the well-groomed English prisoner aboard the *Kincaid*—and a nobleman! Only during his flight up the Ugambi had Lady Greystoke told him the identity of the *Kincaid's* prisoners.

The fight was ending. The African had fought fiercely and refused to surrender even when helpless. There was a quick, unpleasant *snap!* The Swede saw the Englishman leap to his feet beside the corpse of his foe, place one foot on the broken neck, and cut loose with the wild challenge of the victorious bull-ape.

Anderssen shuddered. Then Tarzan turned toward him, murder in his gray eyes.

"Where is my wife?" growled the ape-man.

"Where is the child?"

Anderssen tried to reply, but a sudden fit of coughing choked him with a torrent of blood. There was an arrow entirely through his chest. Tarzan stood, wanting to wring all possible information from this man before killing him.

Presently the coughing ceased, and again the wounded man tried to speak. Tarzan knelt near the faintly moving lips.

"The woman and child!" he repeated. "Where are they?"

Anderssen pointed up the trail.

"The Russian—he got them," he whispered.

"How did you come here?" continued Tarzan. "Why are you not with Rokoff?"

"They catch us," replied Anderssen faintly. "Ay fight, but my men they all run away. Then they get me vhen Ay ben vounded. Rokoff he say leave me here for the hyenas. That vas vorse than to kill. He tak your vife and kid."

"What were you doing with them?" demanded Tarzan fiercely, eyes blazing with fury he could barely control. "What harm did you do to my wife or child? Speak quick before I kill you! Make your peace with God! Tell me, or I will tear you to pieces with my hands and teeth!"

A look of wide-eyed surprise overspread Anderssen's face.

"Vhy," he whispered, "Ay did not hurt them. Ay tried to save them from that Russian. Your vife

vas kind to me on the *Kincaid*, and Ay hear that
little baby cry sometimes. Ay got a vife an' kid for
my own back in Christiania. Ay couldn't bear for
to see them separated an' in Rokoff's hands any
more. That vas all. Do Ay look like Ay ben here to
hurt them?" he continued after a pause, pointing
to the arrow protruding from his chest.

Something in the man's tone and expression
rang true to Tarzan. The man sounded more hurt
than frightened; he knew he was going to die, so
Tarzan's threats on his life meant little. The Swede
seemed to want his captor to know the truth and
not judge him wrongly. The ape-man instantly
dropped to his knees beside the Swede.

"I am sorry," he said. "I had looked for only
evil men in company with Rokoff. I see that I was
wrong. Now we must take care of your wounds
and get you back on your feet again."

The Swede, smiling, shook his head.

"You go on an' look for the vife an' kid," he
said. "Ay ben as gude as dead already; but"—he
hesitated—"Ay hate to tink of the hyenas. Von't
you finish up this job?"

Tarzan shuddered. A moment ago he had
been ready to kill this man. Now he could do
nothing of the kind. He lifted the Swede's head in
his arms to comfort him.

Another bloody coughing fit came. After it
was over Anderssen lay with closed eyes.

Tarzan thought him dead, until he suddenly

raised his eyes to those of the ape-man, sighed, and spoke in a very low, weak whisper:

"Ay tink it blow purty soon purty hard!" he said, and died.

11

Tambudza

Before continuing the pursuit of Rokoff, Tarzan scooped a shallow grave for the *Kincaid's* cook. He wished he could have done more for the strange man who had given his life for Jane and little Jack.

Now that he was positive that Rokoff had Jane, he moved at top speed. The trail was difficult to follow, with many crisscrossing paths used by various natives and wild beasts. By nightfall he realized he had lost the trail.

Knowing that his beasts would track him by scent, he had left an easy trail for them by brushing often against trees and vines. With darkness came a heavy rain. He waited for morning, but it was still pouring. He pressed on in spite of the weather. The next week of travel was filled with constant, violent rain and windstorms that wiped away the last remnants of Rokoff's trail. He saw no sign of natives, nor of his own pack, which had likely lost his trail in the terrific storms. With clouds obscuring the sun, moon, and stars, there was no way to judge his course accurately in this strange country.

When the sun at last broke through the clouds in the morning of the seventh day, it looked down on an almost frantic ape-man. For the first time in his life, Tarzan of the Apes was lost in the jungle. The timing of this difficulty was especially cruel. What might have happened to his wife and son in that week? Rokoff would be furious at Jane's earlier escape and would believe Tarzan to be close upon his trail. He would see every reason to hasten his evil-minded vengeance and none to delay it.

But which direction to take? Rokoff had left the river in pursuit of Anderssen. Would he continue inland or return to the Ugambi? Canoes could not travel much further up the rapidly narrowing river than the point where the Russian had left it, but if Rokoff had not returned to the river, where had he gone? From the original direction of Anderssen's flight with Jane and the child, the ape-man guessed that the Swede had intended to cross Africa to Zanzibar. Would a coward like Rokoff dare so dangerous a journey? Perhaps so, for the Russian knew what sort of pack was on his trail—led by an ape-man hot for revenge.

In the end Tarzan decided to continue northeast in the general direction of German East Africa, hoping to gain information from natives. On the second day after the rains ended, he came to a village. For some reason, the instant the villagers spotted him, the entire population fled into the jungle. Tarzan chased them. Soon he caught up with a young warrior and surprised him before he could use his weapons. Making a sign of friendship, he began to question the youth:

"Why do your people flee from me? I mean you no harm; I am a friend."

"You are the terrible white devil we were warned about."

"Devil?" asked Tarzan in wonderment. "Who gave this strange warning?"

"The party of white men," replied the frightened young man. "They told us that they were being chased by a great devil with light skin, leading a pack of demons shaped like apes and panthers."

Obviously, Rokoff had been at work. By playing on the natives' fear of the strange and unknown, he meant to complicate Tarzan's travel. "What else did this man say?" asked the ape-man.

"He promised us a fabulous reward if we would kill the devil." The warrior did not add that they had indeed planned to do so, but that fright had overcome them—just as the porters of Rokoff's party had quietly warned them would happen. Tarzan thought of a way to turn the situation to his advantage.

"If your people come back and answer my questions, I promise to do your village no harm," said Tarzan. "Call them."

Noting that the "devil" had so far made no effort to harm him, the young man did so, repeating the ape-man's promise loudly to his hidden fellows. One by one they straggled back into the village, eyeing the "devil" with nervous glances.

The chief, a short, stout fellow with a deceitful expression, was among the first to return to the village. He was M'ganwazam, leader of the Waganwazam. M'ganwazam was tempted to order his people to grab Tarzan and slay him, but Rokoff's words held him back. If this were truly a devil, there might be fierce demons nearby to do his bidding.

From M'ganwazam, Tarzan learned that he had suspected correctly: Rokoff's party was in hasty retreat toward the far East Coast. Due to the Russian's cruel treatment, many of his porters had deserted him; he had hanged five for theft and attempted escape in that very village. From what the Waganwazam had learned from the Russian's remaining African carriers, the rest would soon leave him as well—even those who were quite terrified of Rokoff. M'ganwazam denied that there had been any white woman or child with the Russian's party, but Tarzan did not believe him. The ape-man asked the question from several different angles, but was never able to catch the wily chief contradicting himself.

After considerable haggling, the chief agreed to give Tarzan food. The ape-man then tried to draw out others of the tribe, especially the young man he had captured in the bush, but with M'ganwazam present, none would speak. The ape-man was certain that these people were holding back information about Rokoff, Jane, and the child. He decided to stay in the village overnight in hopes of learning more.

When he announced this intention, M'ganwazam's attitude underwent a surprising change: he became an eager, warm host. Nothing would do but the best hut in the village, from which the chief's eldest wife was evicted. M'ganwazam himself moved to the hut of one of his younger wives. The chief realized that to have this white devil sleeping peacefully indoors would make it much easier to earn Rokoff's reward. Therefore, the chief insisted that Tarzan must be very tired and should rest in the best comfort the village could offer.

As much as the ape-man disliked sleeping in native huts, he hoped to strike up a conversation with one of the younger men. He accepted the old chief's invitation, but with a request: rather than drive the poor old lady out to sleep in the cold, might he share a hut with men his own age? Naturally, the elderly woman appreciated the idea; so did the chief, for it would enable him to surround Tarzan with a gang of chosen assassins. Soon the ape-man was shown to a hut near the village gate. There was to be a dance that evening in honor of a recently returned hunting band, said M'ganwazam, and the young men were to participate. Soon Tarzan was left alone.

As soon as the ape-man was safely installed in the trap, M'ganwazam carefully selected a group of young warriors and told them his plan. None was very enthusiastic, but the chief's word was law. As he whispered his plan to them, the chief's elderly wife hovered nearby to busy herself with the firewood supply—and to learn as much as possible. No one paid her any attention.

Despite the noise of the celebration, Tarzan had slept for an hour or two when a stealthy movement in the hut shocked him awake. The fire in the center had died down to glowing embers, making the darkness even harder to penetrate; yet the ape-man was sure someone was creeping toward him. It was probably not a hut-mate, for he could still hear the cries and drums of the revelers. Who, then?

As the presence came within reach of him, the ape-man bounded lightly to the opposite side of the hut, his spear at the ready.

"Who is it," he asked, "that creeps up on Tarzan of the Apes like a hungry lion out of the darkness?"

"Silence!" replied an old cracked voice. "It is Tambudza—the old woman whom you would not drive out to sleep in the cold night."

"What does Tambudza want of Tarzan of the Apes?" asked the ape-man.

"I have come to repay your kindness to me. These days, no one treats me with respect, but you did. I am here to warn you."

"Warn me of what?"

"M'ganwazam has chosen the young men who are to sleep in the hut with you," replied Tambudza. "I heard it all. When the dance is done, they are to come here; if you are asleep, they will simply kill you. If you are awake, they will pretend to be asleep until you are sleeping, then do the same. M'ganwazam is determined to win the reward the white man has offered."

"I had forgotten the reward," said Tarzan, half to himself, and then he added, "How can M'ganwazam collect the reward, if my enemies have left this country and gone who knows where?"

"Oh, they have not gone far," replied Tambudza. "M'ganwazam knows where they camp. His runners could quickly overtake them— they move slowly, and the whites do not know the jungle."

"Where are they?" asked Tarzan.

"Do you wish to find them?" asked Tambudza.

Tarzan nodded.

"Then I will lead you to them."

As they spoke, neither noticed a little figure creeping into the shadows behind them, nor did they see it sneak noiselessly out again. It was little

Buulaoo, the chief's son by one of his younger wives. Buulaoo was a vindictive little tattletale who hated Tambudza and was always trying to get her in trouble with his father.

"Come, then," said Tarzan quickly, "let us be on our way."

This Buulaoo did not hear, for he was already hurrying to where his father sat watching the frantic leaping and cavorting of the wild dance. Thus, as Tarzan and Tambudza sneaked warily from the village and melted into the jungle night, two swift runners headed off in the same direction by another trail.

When they were far enough from the village that it was safe for them to speak above a whisper, Tarzan asked the old woman if she had seen a white woman and a little child.

"Yes," replied Tambudza, "there was a woman with them, carrying a little child. It died here in our village of the fever and was buried!"

12

The Sacrifice

When Jane Clayton looked up from her grief, there was misery and horror in her eyes. She saw Anderssen standing over her with the baby in his arms. "Where is my baby?" she cried.

Anderssen held out the chubby infant, but she shook her head. "It is not mine," she said. "You knew that it was not mine. You are as bad as the Russian."

Anderssen's blue eyes stretched in surprise. "Not yours!" he exclaimed. "You tole me the kid aboard the *Kincaid* ben your kid."

"It isn't," replied Jane dully. "There must have been two; I didn't know about this one. Where is the other?"

"There vasn't no other kid. Ay tink this ben yours. Ay am very sorry." He stared at the ground, looking confused and unhappy. Jane believed him.

Presently the baby made a happy sound, and the Swede bounced him gently up and down in his arms. Little hands reached out toward the young woman. Her motherly heart could not ignore the appeal, and with a low cry she sprang to her feet and gathered the baby close. For a few minutes she wept silently, her face buried in the baby's clothing. The first shock of disappointment was giving way to a great hope: perhaps, somehow, Rokoff had not taken her baby aboard the *Kincaid* at all. Jack might be safe somewhere! Cradling the baby was comforting. Some of the Mosulas smiled; they might not understand English, but they understood motherhood.

"Do you have any idea whose child this is?" she asked Anderssen.

He shook his head. "Not now," he said. "If he ain't ben your kid, Ay don' know whose kid he ben. Rokoff said it was yours. Ay tink he tink so, too. Vhat do we do vith it now? Ay can't go back to the *Kincaid;* Rokoff vould shoot me. But you can go back. Ay take you to the sea, and ve get natives to take you to the ship—eh?"

"No!" cried Jane. "I would rather die than fall into Rokoff's hands again. No, we must take this poor little creature with us. If God is willing, we will be rescued somehow."

So the group resumed their flight, with the half-dozen Mosulas carrying the supplies and tents Anderssen had smuggled aboard the small boat. The days and nights were torture for the young woman, and she lost track of time. Her one comfort was the little baby who had won her heart. It could never truly fill the aching void, but her mother-love for it grew day by day. Sometimes she sat with her eyes closed, imagining that it was her own baby.

Their progress was slow. From time to time they met natives on hunting trips. From them they learned that Rokoff had not yet found their trail. To make the journey as easy as possible on Jane, Anderssen moved at a slow pace with many rests. He insisted on carrying the child while they were moving and did his best to help Jane conserve her strength.

He continued to blame himself for not knowing this was not her child. But Jane insisted that he must not, for he could not have known. At the end of each day, he saw to it that she and the child got the best food and had the best shelter. His gentle consideration and courtesy touched her. She marveled that such an ugly exterior could contain such a kind heart, and soon he no longer seemed repulsive at all.

They were making a little better progress when natives informed them that Rokoff was on their trail and gaining on them. Anderssen bartered with a village chief for a canoe. In it they fled up the broad Ugambi. Soon they no longer received word of their pursuers. Where the river became too shallow for the canoe, they left it and took to the jungle. Here their progress became more difficult and dangerous.

The second day after leaving the Ugambi, the baby fell ill with fever. Anderssen knew how it must end, but he did not have the heart to tell Jane. She had come to love the child almost as if it had been her own flesh and blood. Soon the baby's worsening condition required them to halt, so Anderssen and the Mosula built a camp in a natural clearing on the bank of a little river off the main trail. Here Jane devoted her every moment to caring for the tiny sufferer.

As if things were not already bad enough, a Mosula porter came back from the jungle with awful news: Rokoff and his party were camped nearby. He had evidently found their trail despite Anderssen's best efforts to throw him off their track. They must break camp and move on regardless of the baby's condition. Jane Clayton knew the traits of the Russian all too well: he would surely take the baby away from her, and that would seal its fate.

Soon the Mosula porters began to desert them. They had been staunchly loyal and helpful, but they had also heard about Rokoff's cruelty and had no desire to experience it firsthand. Before long Jane, the Swede, and the baby were traveling all alone, with Jane carrying the child so that Anderssen could hack a way through the brush.

They marched all day, but late that afternoon they heard the noise of a large group close behind them. The freshly cut trail had not only been easy to follow but had also enabled Rokoff to catch up to them quickly. When it became evident that they would soon be overtaken, Anderssen hid Jane behind a large tree, covering her and the child with brush.

"Before they left, the Mosula told me of a village about a mile farther on," he said to her. "Ay try to lead the Russian off your trail, then you go on to the village. Ay tink the chief ben friendly to vhites—the Mosula say so. Anyhow, that is all ve can do. After vhile you get chief to take you down by the Mosula village at the sea again, an' after a vhile a ship is sure to put into the mouth of the Ugambi. Then you be all right. Gude-by an' gude luck to you, lady!"

"But where are you going, Sven?" asked Jane. "Why can't you hide here and go back to the sea with me?"

"Ay gotta tell the Russian you ben dead, so he don't look for you no more," Anderssen grinned.

"Why can't you rejoin me after you have told him that?" insisted Jane.

Anderssen shook his head. "Ay don't tink Ay join anybody any more after Ay tell the Russian you ben dead," he said.

"You don't mean that he will kill you?" asked Jane, and yet in her heart she knew that that was exactly what the great scoundrel would do by way of revenge. Anderssen did not reply, other than to warn her to silence and point toward the path along which they had just come.

"I don't care," whispered Jane Clayton. "I will not let you die to save me if I can prevent it. Give me your revolver. Together we may be able to hold them off until we can escape."

"It von't vork, lady," replied Anderssen. "They vould only get us both, and then Ay couldn't do you no gude at all. Think of the kid, lady; for his sake you must do vhat Ay say. Here, take my rifle; you may need it."

He shoved the gun and an ammunition belt into the shelter beside Jane. Then he was gone.

She watched him double-back to meet the Russian's party. Soon a turn in the trail hid him from view.

Her first impulse was to follow him. With the rifle she might be able to help him, and she could not bear the terrible thought of being left alone in the fearful jungle. She started to crawl from her shelter, intending to run after Anderssen as fast as she could. As she drew the baby close to her she glanced down into its little face.

How red it was! She raised the cheek to hers. It was fiery hot with fever.

With a little gasp of terror Jane Clayton rose to her feet on the jungle path. The rifle and ammunition lay forgotten in the shelter beside her. Anderssen too was forgotten, along with Rokoff, and her dangerous situation; she thought only of her inability to relieve the infant's suffering. If only she could find someone to help her—some woman with children of her own! Then she remembered the friendly village Anderssen had mentioned. Could she reach it in time?

There was no time to lose. Like a startled antelope she turned and fled up the trail in the direction Anderssen had indicated.

From far behind came the sudden shouting, the sound of shots, and then silence. She knew that Anderssen had met the Russian, and knowing the likely result, wept for a good and brave man as she hastened through the jungle.

A half-hour later she stumbled, exhausted, into a little village of thatched huts. Instantly she was surrounded by men, women, and children. They had a hundred curious questions she could not understand, let alone answer; she could only point tearfully at the baby, now wailing piteously in her arms, and repeat over and over, "Fever—fever—fever."

The villagers did not understand her words, but they saw the cause of her trouble. A young woman took pity on her. She and several others took Jane and the baby into a hut where they tried to comfort the baby. The shaman was summoned. He began to boil a strange concoction in a small earthen pot, chanting and gesturing. Presently he dipped a zebra's tail into the brew, and with further mutterings and incantations sprinkled a few drops of the liquid over the baby's face.

After he had gone, the women sat about and moaned and wailed. The noise drove Jane to distraction, but she realized that it was their custom and that it was motivated by their kindness. She endured it in silence.

Toward midnight, she heard a commotion in the village. She heard native voices raised in argument, but she could not understand the words. A few moments later she heard someone approaching the hut.

The little baby lay very still now, its tiny eyes horribly upturned. She had given it all her love, but now she feared that the end was near. All she could hope for was a painless end to the little victim's suffering.

The footsteps halted outside the hut. There were whispers, and a moment later M'ganwazam, chief of the tribe, entered. She had seen little of him because the women had taken her in almost as soon as she had entered the village. The chief had an evil look about him. He tried to talk to her, but she did not understand. Finally, he gave an order to someone outside the hut. Another African entered, a stout warrior who looked and dressed differently from M'ganwazam; she realized that he must be from another tribe. The chief's questioning resumed, with this new arrival as interpreter.

Why was the chief suddenly so interested in her plans? The questions made her suspicious, especially those about where she had been headed when she came to his village. However, she saw no reason to withhold the truth, and so she told him.

When he asked if she expected to meet her husband at the end of the trip, she shook her head in the negative. Then, through the interpreter, the chief told her why he had asked her these questions:

• "I have just learned," he said, "from some men who live near the great water, that your husband followed you up the Ugambi some distance, but was ambushed and killed by natives. So, just in case you were intending to meet your husband, this information may save you a long journey. You may wish to turn back toward the coast."

Jane thanked M'ganwazam for his advice, though her heart felt new pain at this terrible news. It was just one more misery in a long series of sorrows, a sharp pang against a background of constant dull aching. With bowed head, she stared blankly at the face of the baby in her lap as M'ganwazam left the hut.

Some time later she heard someone else enter the hut. One of the women sitting opposite her threw a bundle of sticks onto the dying embers of the fire. The burst of renewed flame lit up the hut's interior as though by magic.

In the light of the flame, Jane Clayton saw to her horror that the baby was dead; she could not guess for how long. A choking lump rose to her throat. She gripped the lifeless little bundle to her chest, laid her head upon it in silent misery, and wept inside.

For a moment the hut was quiet. Then the

young woman who had taken pity on her when she first arrived broke into a terrible wail.

Close in front of Jane Clayton, a man coughed and spoke her name. With a start, she raised her eyes. Above her was an evil face she knew far too well.

It was none other than Nikolai Rokoff.

13

Escape

For a moment Rokoff sneered down at Jane Clayton. Then his eyes fell to the little bundle in her lap. Jane had drawn one corner of the blanket over the child's face, so that it appeared to be sleeping.

"You wasted a lot of effort," said Rokoff, "by bringing the child to this village. If you had minded your business I would have brought it here myself. I guess I owe you thanks, at least, for saving me the trouble of caring for it. From here, M'ganwazam will raise him to be a good African warrior, and if you ever get home, you will have much leisure to compare your own luxuries with his life here. And now, it is time for his foster parents to receive him." Rokoff held out his hands for the child, grinning nastily.

To his surprise, Jane Clayton rose and laid the little bundle in his arms without protest.

"Here is the child," she said. "Thank God he is beyond your power to harm him."

Rokoff snatched the blanket from the child's face. Jane watched his expression closely, for she had wondered whether Rokoff knew the baby's true identity. When he saw that his revenge had been thwarted, his terrible burst of anger erased all doubt. He practically threw the poor infant's body

back into her arms, then stomped up and down the hut, pounding the air with clenched fists as he cursed and swore. At last he leaned down into Jane's face and shrieked:

"You are laughing at me! You think that you have beaten me, eh? I'll show you, as I have shown the miserable ape you call 'husband,' what it means to interfere with the plans of Nikolai Rokoff. Your child will not live out his life in this village, but after I finish with you,"—he paused to let the full impact sink in— "I'll bring you back here and leave you to live out *your* life in this village. I'm sure you will enjoy that."

If he had meant to frighten her, he failed miserably. She was numb to suffering and shock. Instead she smiled faintly, almost happily: the dead child was not her own little Jack, and better still, Rokoff obviously did not know it. Her son might be alive and maybe even safe. Perhaps one of the Russian's henchmen had betrayed him and ransomed the child in London. If so, Jack's odds were good. She had many friends in London who would have willingly paid any sum demanded for the safe release of Lord Greystoke's son.

She resisted the urge to taunt him with the fact that this was not her child, for in Rokoff's ignorance lay Jack's only hope. Her own position was hopeless. With Anderssen and her husband dead, no one would have any idea where to find her. Rokoff's threat meant only an earlier release from her suffering because she would commit suicide before the Russian could harm her further. If she could not find a way back to her own child, she did not care to live—but she was not yet ready to choose between Nikolai Rokoff and suicide.

"Go away!" she said to the Russian. "Leave me in peace with my dead child. Have you not already brought me enough misery? What wrong have I ever done to you to make you keep tormenting me?"

"You are suffering for the sins of the ape-man you preferred over me, a refined gentleman," he snarled. "But there is no more to discuss. We will bury the child here. You are to return with me at once to my camp. Tomorrow I will bring you back to your new home. Come!"

He reached out for the child. Jane got to her feet and turned away from him.

"I will bury my son," she said. "Send some men to dig a grave outside the village."

Rokoff was anxious to get back to his camp with his victim. Believing she had accepted her fate, he motioned her to follow him outside the hut. He and his men escorted Jane beyond the village. Beneath a great tree, the sailors dug a shallow grave.

Jane wrapped the tiny body in a blanket and laid it tenderly to rest. Turning her head so that she would not see the earth falling upon the pitiful little bundle, she breathed a prayer beside the grave of the nameless little one. Then, saddened beyond tears, she rose and followed the Russian to his encampment.

They disappeared along the long, leafy corridor into the jungle, serenaded by the sounds of hunting beasts snarling and roaring. Rokoff urged them to greater speed in a quavering voice. The noises of the jungle night reminded her vividly of happier days in a similar jungle with her forest god, the fearless and unconquerable Tarzan of the Apes. Then there had been no terror at all. Then the roar of a lion had seemed the most awesome sound on earth. If only Tarzan were somewhere in this jungle, seeking her, there would be every reason to hope for rescue—but he was dead.

The thought was incredible. That great body and its mighty muscles seemed immortal. If it had been Rokoff who told her of her husband's death, she would have known it was a lie, but she could think of no reason for M'ganwazam to have deceived her. She did not know that the Russian had talked with M'ganwazam a few minutes before the chief had brought her the story.

At last they reached the wall of thorny brush ringing the Russian's camp. The camp was in turmoil. She did not know what it was about, but Rokoff was infuriated. From bits of conversation she could translate, she determined that more of the Africans had deserted—taking most of the food and ammunition with them. Two of the sailors guarded Jane while Rokoff heaped profanity upon the remaining native carriers. When he was done, he returned to Jane, grasped her roughly by the arm, and started to haul her toward his tent.

She struggled and fought to free herself as the sailors laughed at her desperate situation. Rokoff ended her struggles by slugging her repeatedly in the face until she was stunned. Then he dragged her inside.

Rokoff's servant lit a lamp, then obeyed his master's snarled order to get out. Jane was on the floor in the middle of the shelter. Her senses were returning, and she began to think quickly, taking inventory of all she could see while pretending to be unconscious. Of special interest to her was a huge revolver at her enemy's belt. Rokoff wrapped his loathsome arms around her and began to drag her toward the camp cot. She waited for her chance to grab the weapon. The gun was so close to her fingers, they itched.

The opportunity came just as Rokoff was lifting her onto the cot. A noise at the entrance to the tent made him turn away from her. The butt of the gun was an inch from her hand. With a single swift move she snatched the weapon from its holster. She dared not fire, for it would bring the sailors— and to judge by the way they had laughed while she was beaten, their hands might be even less gentle than Rokoff's.

As the angry, frightened face of the Russian turned toward her, Jane Clayton brought the heavy revolver far back, and with all her strength she dealt the man a terrific blow between the eyes.

Rokoff crumpled silently to the ground. A moment later the woman stood beside his motionless figure—safe, at least for a moment, from the menace of his lust.

She again heard the noise outside the tent that had distracted Rokoff. Afraid she would be discovered, she stepped quickly to the camp table and put out the smoky oil lamp. In total darkness, she paused to collect her wits and plan her next step toward freedom.

All around her was a camp of enemies. Beyond that lay a savage jungle filled with hideous beasts of prey. She doubted that she could survive even a few days in the jungle, but she had already survived many perils. More importantly, somewhere far away, a little child needed her. Jane steeled herself: she must cross this frightful land, reach the sea, and hope for the remote possibility of aid.

Rokoff's tent stood almost exactly in the center of the camp, surrounded by the tents and shelters of the sailors and carriers. Escape seemed impossible, but she must try, for to stay here would mean certain discovery. With that thought, she approached the back of the tent to begin this new adventure.

Groping along the rear of the canvas wall, she found that it had no opening. Quickly she returned to the side of the unconscious Russian, and fumbling at his belt, she found the hilt of a long hunting knife. She drew it and stepped quietly to the back wall, where she slit a long vertical hole.

Silently she stepped outside. To her immense relief, the camp was asleep. In the flickering light of the dying fires, she saw only a single dozing sentry at the far side, near the entrance to the protective wall of thorny brush that encircled the camp.

Keeping the tent between him and herself, she crossed between the small shelters of the native porters to the wall beyond. Outside she could hear the roaring of lions, the laughing of hyenas, and the countless, nameless noises of the jungle night.

For a moment she hesitated, trembling. Then, with a sudden brave toss of her head, she attacked the thorny wall with her delicate hands. Though her hands were soon torn and bleeding, she worked on breathlessly until she had made an opening she could squeeze through. At last she stood outside the enclosure.

Behind her lay a fate worse than death, at the hands of human beings.

Before her lay an almost certain fate, but it was only death: sudden, merciful, and honorable.

Without regret she darted away from the camp. The mysterious jungle closed around her.

14

Alone in the Jungle

Tambudza, slowed by her age and rheumatism, led Tarzan of the Apes toward Rokoff's camp. The runners sent to warn the Russian that the white giant would soon be slain in their village reached Rokoff before Tarzan and his ancient guide had covered half the distance.

When the runners arrived, the camp was in chaos. That morning, Rokoff had been found stunned and bleeding inside his tent. When he realized that Jane Clayton had escaped, he went berserk. At first he rushed about the camp with his rifle, intending to shoot the African sentry who had been so careless as to let her escape. Several of the other whites, however, realized what a suicidal move this would be, so they seized and disarmed him. Their party had already suffered enough desertions thanks to Rokoff's cruelty.

Then came the messengers from M'gan-wazam, but just as Rokoff was preparing to depart with them, two other runners came panting into the camp. One shouted: "The great white giant has escaped from M'ganwazam! He and his pack of demons will kill us all!"

This brought new confusion to the camp. Rokoff's few remaining African carriers had had enough. Being eaten for sure by a fierce pack of apes and panthers was far worse than maybe being shot by Rokoff. They—and M'ganwazam's messengers—quickly grabbed anything of value they could get their hands on. All of them scurried into the bush, leaving Rokoff and the seven white sailors deserted and robbed in the midst of a wilderness.

Naturally, the Russian began to yell at his companions, blaming them for the entire mess, but the sailors were tired of his insults and curses. One drew a revolver and fired it at Rokoff. He somehow missed, and Rokoff turned and fled to his tent.

As he ran he happened to look beyond the enclosing wall to the edge of the forest, and there he caught a glimpse of something. The sight was even more terrifying to him than the sailors, who by now were all firing in hate and revenge at his retreating back.

He saw the giant figure of an almost-naked white man emerging from the bush.

Darting into his tent, the Russian kept right on going through the rear wall, taking advantage of the long slit that Jane Clayton had made the night before. Like a hunted rabbit, the terrified Russian pushed through the still-gaping hole that Jane had made in the thorny fence. As Tarzan approached the camp from the opposite side, Rokoff disappeared into the jungle.

As the ape-man entered the camp with old Tambudza at his elbow, the seven sailors recognized him and fled past him and into the jungle. Seeing that Rokoff was not among them, he ignored them and headed for Rokoff's tent. Tarzan knew that the jungle would give these villains what they deserved. He was right, for their fate is known only to Africa, and Africa will not tell.

Finding Rokoff's tent empty, Tarzan was about to pursue the Russian when Tambudza had a suggestion: the evil man's departure must have resulted from word reaching him from M'ganwazam that Tarzan was in his village.

"He must be headed there," said the old woman. "Let us return at once."

This made sense, so Tarzan set out briskly for the village of M'ganwazam, leaving Tambudza to follow at her own slow pace. His one hope was that Jane was still safe and with Rokoff. If so, he should soon be able to get her back. He knew now to expect treachery from M'ganwazam; he might have to fight to rescue his wife. He wished that Mugambi, Sheeta, Akut, and the rest of the pack were with him. It would not be easy to bring Jane safely out of the clutches of two such scoundrels as Rokoff and the wily chief.

To his surprise he found no sign of either Rokoff or Jane in the village. He did not trust M'ganwazam's word, so he wasted no time asking questions. Before the chief could even try to prevent him from leaving, he vanished into the jungle like a well-thrown African spear.

Swinging through the trees, he hastened back to the deserted camp of Rokoff to find the trail of Rokoff and Jane. Moving along the outer perimeter of the enclosure, he came to a break in the thorny wall. Something had recently passed through. A moment later he was through the wall and following the faint trail.

Far ahead of him a terror-stricken young woman was slinking along a narrow game-trail, fearful that the next moment would bring her face to face with doom. As she ran, hoping desperately that this was the way to the great river, she stumbled on a familiar spot.

At one side of the trail, beneath a giant tree, lay a little heap of loosely piled brush. To her dying day, she would never forget that little spot of jungle. This was where Anderssen had hidden her, then sacrificed his life to try and save her from Rokoff. Here, forgotten until now, were the rifle and ammunition the Swede had given her. While she still had Rokoff's revolver, it could not contain more than six shots, maybe less—hardly enough to furnish her with food and protection on the long journey. It was with relief and joy that her fingers found the barrel of the heavy weapon, along with its ammunition belt. Slinging the belt over her shoulder and taking the rifle in her hands, she felt new confidence and optimism. She returned to the path with bolder strides.

That night she slept in the fork of a tree, as Tarzan had so often described, and early the next morning was moving again. Late in the afternoon, as she was about to cross a little clearing, she was startled to see a huge ape coming from the jungle on the opposite side.

The wind was blowing between them, and Jane quickly put herself downwind from the huge creature. Then she hid in a clump of heavy bushes and watched, holding the rifle ready for instant use. More apes were gathering in the clearing, and as if that were not worrisome enough, they looked around as though waiting for others. Jane wished that they would go on, for any change in wind direction might carry her scent to them. What good would the rifle be against them all?

Her eyes moved back and forth between the apes and the edge of the jungle toward which they were gazing. Finally she saw why they had halted: they were being stalked. Sure enough, there was the lithe form of a panther, gliding out of the jungle where the apes had emerged into the clearing.

Quickly the beast trotted toward the apes. To Jane's wonder, they seemed not to care. Her wonder increased tenfold when the great cat went right up to the apes—who did not react—and began to groom itself like an overgrown house cat.

If Jane was surprised by the sight of these natural enemies fraternizing, the next event made her wonder if she had lost her mind. A tall, muscular African warrior entered the clearing and joined the animals. At first she raised her rifle, hoping to save the man from becoming the beasts' lunch, but nothing of the sort happened. In fact, he seemed to be giving them orders!

Presently the entire company filed on across the clearing and disappeared in the jungle on the opposite side.

With a gasp of mingled incredulity and relief Jane Clayton got to her feet and headed away from the fearsome horde. A half-mile behind her, Rokoff lay frozen with terror behind an anthill as the band passed quite close to him. Unlike Jane, however, he had recognized the allies of Tarzan of the Apes. No sooner had they passed than he rose and raced through the jungle as fast as he could go in the other direction.

And so, when Jane Clayton came to the bank of the river, Nikolai Rokoff was close on her heels. To her great joy, she saw a great dugout canoe moored to a tree nearby. If she could manage to launch the huge craft, her transportation difficulties would be solved. She was able to untie the rope, but when she climbed into the canoe and tried to shove off, she found that the sturdy vessel's bow was firmly stuck in the mud of the bank. She pushed with all her might, but it would not move.

Then Jane had another idea: she would load the stern with weight, then rock the bow back and forth along the bank until the craft eventually worked itself into the river. There were no stones close by, but there was plenty of driftwood. She piled it into the stern. To her immense relief, the bow rose gently from the mud of the bank. The stern drifted a bit, then lodged a little farther downstream. Jane found that by running back and forth between the bow and stern she could alternately raise and lower each end of the boat. Each time she leaped to the stern, the canoe edged farther into the river.

So closely was she focused on her work that she failed to notice the figure of a man standing beneath a huge tree at the edge of the jungle. He watched her labors with a malicious grin.

The boat was nearly clear of the muddy bank now, and Jane felt ready to push it free with one of the paddles. She seized one and plunged it into the river—and as she did so, she spotted movement in the brush.

A little cry of terror rose to her lips. It was Rokoff. He ran toward her, telling her to wait or he would shoot—though he was entirely unarmed, so it was a meaningless threat.

Jane Clayton knew nothing of the Russian's troubles since she had escaped from his tent, so she believed that his followers must also be nearby. She knew she would rather die than fall into his hands again. Another minute and the boat would be free—and so would she, for no man, especially not the cowardly Rokoff, would dare leap into the crocodile-infested water after her.

Rokoff, for his part, was interested only in escape at this moment. He would gladly have abandoned any evil designs on Jane Clayton, promised anything, if she would share this means of escape with him. He realized that he would not have to make her any promises, however, for he saw that he could easily reach the bow with his hand. He was pleased, for the notion of begging a favor from her was distasteful. Already he was gloating over the days and nights of revenge he would savor while the heavy dugout drifted slowly down toward the ocean.

Jane Clayton, shoving furiously with the paddle, felt the boat give way. With a little lurch the dugout swung quickly into the current just as the Russian reached out to grasp its bow. His fingers missed it by inches. Heaving a great sigh of relief, she began to relax into the boat to rest from the terrific mental and physical strain of the past few minutes and to give thanks for her escape.

Even as she breathed her silent prayer, she saw

a sudden expression of triumph lighten the features of the cursing Russian. He dropped suddenly to the ground, grasping something that wriggled through the mud toward the water.

Jane Clayton watched in horror from the bottom of the boat. At the last instant, success had turned to failure, and she was again in the power of the spiteful Rokoff.

The Russian was grasping the loose end of the rope that had moored the dugout to the tree.

15

Down the Ugambi

Halfway between the Ugambi and the village of the Waganwazam, Tarzan rediscovered the pack. He studied the trail with Mugambi, and after some discussion they agreed that both the man and woman had hidden as the pack passed, but were not traveling together. It appeared that Rokoff had started out far behind Jane but had gained rapidly.

The reunited pack followed the trail to the river, with Tarzan leaping out ahead. At the bank, there were the two sets of footprints, and the imprint of a canoe's bow, but no sign of the vessel or of the footprints' owners. Plainly the two had gotten into the native canoe. As the ape-man's eye ran swiftly downriver, he saw movement in the distance.

A drifting dugout was just rounding a bend and passing from view. A man was sitting in the stern.

Mugambi and the rest arrived at the river to see their agile leader racing down the bank, leaping over the swampy ground that spread between them and the point where the river curved out of their sight. The heavy apes had to make a wide detour around the swampy ground, as did Sheeta, who hated the water. Mugambi followed as swiftly as he could.

A half-hour of rapid travel brought Tarzan to the inward bend of the winding river. There before him in mid-stream was the dugout with Nikolai Rokoff in its stern.

Without Jane.

At sight of his enemy, the broad scar upon the ape-man's brow burned scarlet, and he bellowed the deadly challenge of the bull-ape.

Rokoff shuddered at the terrible sound and cowered into the bottom of the boat. With chattering teeth he watched his worst nightmare run quickly to the water's edge. Fear gave way to frantic hysteria in the Russian's heart as the giant dove unafraid into the forbidding waters of the tropical river. With steady, powerful strokes the ape-man swam for the drifting dugout, and Rokoff began to paddle frantically for his life.

And from the opposite bank a sinister ripple, unseen by either man, moved steadily toward the half-naked swimmer.

Tarzan had reached the stern of the craft at last. One hand grasped the side. Rokoff sat frozen with fear, his eyes riveted on the face of his hunter rising above the boat's side.

Then a sudden commotion in the water behind the swimmer caught his attention. He saw the ripple, and he knew what caused it.

At the same instant Tarzan felt mighty jaws close on his right leg. He tried to struggle free and climb into the boat, and would have succeeded but for the Russian's quick thinking. Like a snake, Rokoff leaped up and dealt Tarzan a swift and violent blow across the head with the heavy paddle. The ape-man's fingers slipped from their hold on the boat.

There was a short struggle at the surface, and then a swirl of waters and a little eddy. Then a burst of bubbles soon smoothed out by the flowing current. This last sign momentarily marked the spot where Tarzan of the Apes, Lord of the Jungle, disappeared from the sight of men beneath the gloomy waters of the dark and forbidding Ugambi.

Weak from terror, Rokoff sank shuddering into the bottom of the dugout. For a moment he could not realize his good fortune—all he could see was his struggling enemy going down to a muddy, watery grave. As the meaning of it filtered into his mind, a cruel smile of relief and triumph came to his lips. It was short-lived.

Just as he was looking forward to a safe trip downriver, a frightful commotion rose from the nearby riverbank. Rokoff looked toward it and saw what he dreaded most.

Standing on the shore were a devil-faced panther, the hideous apes of Akut, and a giant African warrior, all with murder in their eyes. The African shook his fist and shouted. Had Rokoff understood his language, he would have been even more frightened at the revenge Mugambi promised.

Rokoff's flight down the Ugambi was a nightmare, for the tireless Mugambi and the beasts pursued him without end, day and night. They would nearly catch up to him, then fall behind, delayed by the tangled jungle, then reappear. The Russian who had boarded the canoe had been a strong, healthy man. The constant fear of the trip soon reduced him to a skinny, white-haired, insane creature. As he fled past villages, warriors launched canoes to intercept him, but when Mugambi and the beasts came into view, the warriors thought better of it and got out of their way.

There was no sight of Jane Clayton. After Rokoff had grabbed the rope of her canoe, the idea that she was in his power once more had quickly been driven from his mind. She had picked up a heavy hunting rifle and leveled it at his heart. Rokoff had dropped the rope in a hurry, and had to watch helplessly as she floated beyond his reach. He had raced upstream toward a little tributary river where he and the sailors had landed their canoe to chase Jane and Anderssen inland.

What had become of her? Captured, most probably, or fallen overboard. Either way, at least he was rid of most of his human enemies—but he would have rather had them all than the enemies who were chasing him now. The most terrifying was the panther, the flaming-eyed cat whose grinning jaws gaped wide at him by day, and whose fiery orbs gleamed wickedly out across the water from the dark jungle nights.

The sight of the mouth of the Ugambi renewed Rokoff's hope. There floated the *Kincaid* at anchor. He had sent the little steamer away to refuel with coal while he had gone upriver, leaving Paulvitch in charge of the ship. He paddled furiously toward her, now and then waving and calling out in hopes of getting someone's attention. No one answered. He gave a hurried backward glance; ashore, behind him, he saw the snarling pack. Even now, he thought, the African and the animals might find a way to chase him up to the steamer's deck. Those on board would need to be ready to drive them back with gunfire.

What could have happened to those he had left on board the *Kincaid*? Where was Paulvitch? Was he doomed to be overtaken by the terrible fate he had flown from all these horrible days and nights? As he sensed the clammy fingers of death reaching for him, he shivered and kept paddling frantically for the steamer.

After what seemed like forever, the heavy bow of the dugout bumped against the timbers of the *Kincaid*. Over the ship's side hung a rope ladder, but as the Russian grasped it, a feminine voice from above ordered him to halt. He looked up into the cold, steady muzzle of a rifle.

After Jane Clayton had kept Rokoff from boarding her canoe at rifle-point, her vessel had drifted beyond the Russian's reach into the Ugambi. She had quickly paddled it to the swiftest part of the river, and had spent weary days and nights working to keep it there. Only during the hottest hours of the day had she rested and let the current take her as it wished. At those times, she lay in the bottom of the boat with a great palm leaf as a sunshade. At all other times, she had sped her movement by use of the paddle.

Rokoff, on the other hand, had used little or no energy or intelligence in his trip down-stream. More often than not his craft had drifted in the slow-moving eddies. He paddled only enough to keep the canoe near the opposite bank from his relentless pursuers. Jane had reached the bay two hours ahead of him.

When she had first seen the anchored ship on the quiet water, Jane Clayton's heart had beaten fast with hope, but as she drew closer to the craft and saw that it was the *Kincaid*, her hope gave way to worry. In any event, it had been too late to turn back. The current that carried her toward the ship was much too strong for her to force the heavy dugout upstream. She could either try to go ashore without being seen by those on the ship, or throw herself on their mercy. If she did otherwise, she would be swept out to sea.

The shore held little hope for her. She had no idea how to find the friendly Mosula village where Anderssen had taken her under cover of darkness. With Rokoff away from the steamer, perhaps those on board—being the sorts of low characters likely to associate with Rokoff in the first place—could be bribed to take her to a civilized port. It was worth risking, if she could make it to the steamer. The current was threatening to carry her right past it, and it took all her strength to maneuver the heavy canoe toward the *Kincaid*.

Her decision made, she now looked to the larger vessel for aid, but to her surprise the decks seemed deserted. Her cries for assistance received no reply. In a moment more, Jane realized, the powerful ebb tide would carry her past the ship and far out to sea. For a moment it seemed that she would miss her goal by just a few feet, but at the last moment the canoe swung close beneath the steamer's bow and Jane barely managed to grasp the anchor chain.

She clung heroically to the heavy iron links, almost dragged from the canoe by its momentum. Then, beyond her, she saw a rope ladder dangling over the steamer's side. To let go and hope to catch the ladder as her canoe floated by was a risky option. It also seemed to be her only one.

Then she remembered the rope in the bow of

the dugout. She managed to reach it with one hand without losing her grip with the other, and she passed it through the chain links. Tying one end tightly to the chain, she paid out rope until the canoe lay directly beneath the ladder. A moment later, her rifle slung about her shoulders, she clambered safely to the deserted deck of the *Kincaid*.

Her first task was to investigate the ship, and this she did, her rifle at the ready. It did not take her long to learn why the steamer looked deserted. When she peered into through a glass porthole into the crew's cabin, she saw two sailors sprawled out in a sound sleep. They had evidently been left to guard the ship, and judging by the bottles, they were sleeping off a drunk.

With a shudder of disgust she climbed on top of the cabin and fastened the hatch shut to imprison the sleeping guards. She then went to the galley and found some food. Her hunger satisfied, she took up a position on deck. With the rifle in hand, she was determined not to let anyone aboard except on her own terms.

For an hour or so nothing happened. Then she saw a canoe appear around an upstream bend. A single figure sat in the approaching dugout. It did not take her long to recognize Rokoff, even after his ordeal. When he attempted to board, he found himself at gunpoint.

Rokoff's first tactic was to curse and threaten

her. She remained coldly immune to his bluster, and he soon fell to pleading and promising. To his every proposition, Jane had the same reply: if he tried to come up, she would shoot him dead. Rokoff had no doubt that she meant it. He had no choice but to go back down to his dugout and make for shore. The current nearly carried him out to sea, but finally he succeeded in reaching land far down the bay, on the opposite side from the horde of snarling, roaring beasts and their African leader.

Jane Clayton knew that, by himself, Rokoff could never get the heavy canoe back upstream to the *Kincaid*, so she had no further fear of an attack by him. She recognized the group on the shore as the same that had passed her in the jungle far up the Ugambi several days before. It was impossible that there could be two such packs, but she could not imagine what had brought them here.

Toward the day's end she heard the Russian shouting from the opposite bank of the stream, and a moment later she was terrified to see a ship's boat approaching from upstream. It could only contain members of the *Kincaid's* missing crew. Every one of them was a cruel and heartless ruffian, except for Anderssen—and he was dead.

16

In the Darkness of the Night

In the jaws of a crocodile, most ordinary men would have resigned themselves to fate. Tarzan of the Apes, of course, was no ordinary man.

Instead, he took a deep breath before the huge reptile dragged him underwater and prepared to fight for freedom. Unlike the crocodile, though, he was not in his native element. His struggles only encouraged the monster to move faster, and soon Tarzan's lungs were bursting for a breath of pure fresh air.

He knew that the end was near. If he could not escape, he could at least avenge his own death. With that thought, he drew his stone knife and stabbed at the creature's tough armor. Again the beast moved faster.

Just as the ape-man realized that he was at the limit of his endurance, he felt his body dragged onto a muddy bank and his nostrils rise above water. All about him was dark silence. The great reptile released him.

For a moment Tarzan of the Apes lay gasping for breath on the slimy, evil-smelling bed to which the animal had carried him. Close at his side he could feel the hard plates of the creature's coat rising and falling as though it was struggling to breathe. Mutually exhausted, they lay that way for several minutes. The giant carcass at his side then convulsed, and finally stiffened.

To the ape-man's amazement, the beast was dead. The slim knife had found a vulnerable spot in the scaly armor.

Tarzan's leg was badly torn, but the bone was not broken and there was no apparent muscle or tendon damage. It was painful but usable, and Tarzan of the Apes was used to pain. He gave it no further thought.

Staggering to his feet, the ape-man groped about the reeking, oozy den. As his eyes got used to the darkness, he discovered that he was imprisoned in a great underground cave big enough to house a dozen crocodiles. It must be the creature's hidden nest far beneath the bank of the stream. Undoubtedly, the only way out was the way he had been brought in.

His first thought, of course, was of escape—but could he forge through the dark, silty water to the surface of the river, then to the shore beyond? It seemed unlikely. The tunnel might branch off; worse, he might meet another crocodile in the tunnel or in the river. In any case, there was no alternative, so he filled his lungs with the stale, smelly air of the chamber and dove back into the water.

Both crawling and swimming, he found that the passage inclined downward, then upward. Soon there was faint light from above—he was on the right path. It opened at last into the river bottom a few feet from shore.

As the ape-man reached the surface he saw the heads of two great crocodiles close by, moving rapidly toward him. With a superhuman effort, Tarzan reached for the overhanging branches of a nearby tree. He had barely drawn himself to the safety of the limb when two gaping mouths snapped viciously below him.

For a few minutes Tarzan rested in the tree that had been his salvation. His eyes scanned the river as far downstream as he could see, but there was no sign of the Russian or his dugout.

When he had rested and bound up his wounded leg, he started out after Rokoff's drifting canoe. He was on the other side of the river from where he had entered. However, that detail was less important to him than the painful discovery that the crocodile bite was worse than he had thought. The injury limited him to a walk, and travel through the trees was not merely slower, but highly dangerous.

As he limped along, he remembered something that old Tambudza had told him. After the child had died, the grieving white woman had confided

in her: the baby had not been her own.

The ape-man had his doubts. Why would Jane have denied her identity, or that of the child? He could think of only one explanation: perhaps the woman who had gone into the interior with his son and the Swede had not been Jane at all.

The more thought he gave it, the surer he became that his son was dead and his wife still safe in London, unaware of her first-born's terrible fate. In that case, he had misunderstood the meaning of Rokoff's sinister taunt. This, however, gave him little comfort in his grief over the loss of his baby son, an innocent little child who had perished miserably.

As Tarzan made his way painfully toward the coast, he thought constantly about the Russian's frightful crimes against his loved ones. The broad scar on his forehead stood out almost continuously in the vivid scarlet that marked his fury. At times he let out involuntary roars and growls, sending the lesser creatures of the wild jungle scampering to their hiding places.

If he could only get his hands on the Russian!

Twice on the way to the coast, native warriors ran threateningly from their villages to block his way. Both times, they met with an unworldly white giant giving the awful battle cry of the bull-ape. Both groups had second thoughts and got out of his way.

To Tarzan, whose idea of speed was measured

against that of apes in trees, his progress seemed ridiculously slow. Even so, he was moving about as fast as Rokoff's drifting canoe. He came to the bay just after dark on the same day that Jane Clayton and the Russian had arrived.

It was an especially dark night; even with eyes well accustomed to nighttime use, Tarzan could see little. His idea was to search the shore that night for signs of the Russian and the woman who must have preceded Rokoff down the Ugambi. He had no idea that the *Kincaid*, or any other ship, lay at anchor less than a hundred yards from him.

As he began his search, a sudden noise made him freeze to listen: the stealthy dip of paddles in the water some distance from the shore. Then it ceased, to be followed by a muffled noise that sounded like something bumping up against a boat. And yet, as far as he could see, there was no ship there. There might not be one within a thousand miles.

While he stood peering out into the darkness of the cloud-enshrouded night, sounds came to him like a slap in the face. There were the sharp cracks of rifle fire, then a woman's scream.

In spite of his wounds and the recent memory of a horrible experience, Tarzan of the Apes did not hesitate as the notes of that frightened cry pierced the still night air. With a bound he cleared the bush and splashed into the water, then swam with powerful strokes out into the impenetrable night. He had no guide but the memory of a brief cry, nor any company but the hideous inhabitants of a jungle river.

The boat that Jane had spotted as she stood guard on the deck of the *Kincaid* had also been noticed by Rokoff on one bank and by Mugambi and the horde on the other. The cries of the Russian had brought the dugout first to him; then, after a conference, it had been turned toward the *Kincaid*.

Before it covered half the distance between the shore and the steamer, a rifle had spoken from the ship's deck, and a sailor in the bow of the canoe had crumpled and fallen into the water. After that they went more slowly. When Jane's rifle had found another member of the party, the canoe returned to the shore, where it lay until nightfall.

The savage, snarling pack on the opposite shore was directed by the African warrior, Mugambi, chief of the Wagambi. Among them, only he could distinguish between friend and foe. If the beasts could have reached either the canoe or the *Kincaid*, they would have made short work of anyone they found there. But the span of black water separating them from their prey might as well have been a broad ocean.

Tarzan had told Mugambi about the events leading up to his marooning on Jungle Island. The African knew that the ape-man was trying to rescue his wife and child from the wicked white man who had stolen them. And he knew that it was that wicked white man that they had followed far into the interior and that Mugambi and the pack had now followed back to the sea.

It was hard for Mugambi to believe that he had thought of the ape-man as his savage captor when he first faced him on Jungle Island. Matters certainly had changed: Tarzan was no longer his captor; he had become a friend and partner. Mugambi had come to respect and love him as he had never loved even the greatest chiefs of his own people, and he grieved the death of this great man. His heart burned with iron resolve: to avenge the murder of his friend.

When Mugambi saw the canoe come down the river and take Rokoff aboard, then make for the *Kincaid*, he realized that he must find a canoe in order to transport the pack within striking distance of the enemy. And so, even before Jane Clayton fired the first shot into Rokoff's canoe, the beasts of Tarzan had disappeared into the jungle.

Though the Russian and his party—Paulvitch and the men he had left on the *Kincaid* to handle the refueling—had retreated before her fire, Jane realized that they would be back soon. She decided to make a bold and final stroke for freedom. Opening negotiations with the two sailors she had imprisoned in the cabin, she forced them to agree to her plan. If they betrayed her, she told them, she would shoot them dead. They were released just as darkness closed about the ship.

With her revolver ready to compel obedience, she let them up one at a time, searching them carefully for concealed weapons as they stood with hands up. Once satisfied that they were unarmed, she set them to work hoisting the *Kincaid's* anchor. This would set the steamer adrift into the open sea, where she would trust to the mercy of the elements—which could be no more cruel than Nikolai Rokoff if he were to capture her again.

There was also every reason to hope that some passing ship might sight the *Kincaid*. According to the men, the boat was well stocked with provisions and water. With the storm season well over, many vessels sailed the coast of Africa in both directions.

The night was deeply overcast, heavy clouds riding low above the jungle and the water. Only to the west, where the broad ocean spread beyond the river's mouth, was there a suggestion of lessening gloom.

It was a perfect night for Jane's purposes. Her enemies could not see the activity onboard the ship, nor could they see where the swift current might take her. Before daylight broke, the ebb tide would carry the *Kincaid* well into the Benguela current, which flows northward along the coast of Africa. Jane hoped to be out of sight of the mouth of the Ugambi before Rokoff realized the steamer was gone.

Standing over the laboring seamen, the young woman breathed a sigh of relief as they finished raising the anchor: she knew that the vessel was on its way out to sea. She ordered her prisoners back to the cabin at rifle-point, but both replied with promises of loyalty and usefulness, and pleaded to remain free. Finally Jane was swayed by their arguments, and let them remain on deck.

In the meantime, the *Kincaid* drifted rapidly with the current. Then, with a grinding jar, she stopped in midstream. The ship had struck a low-lying bar in mid-channel, about a quarter mile from the sea.

For a moment she hung there, then swung round slowly until her bow pointed shoreward, and broke adrift once more.

At the same instant, just as Jane Clayton was exulting that the ship was once more free, new sounds came from upriver, near the former anchor-point: the rattle of rifle fire, punctuated by the shrill, terrified scream of a woman.

To the sailors, the gunfire could only mean one thing: their employer was returning. They had accepted Jane's terms because, at that time, they had no other choice. The possibility of Rokoff returning to the ship now gave them another option. They whispered a hurried plan. They would overcome the young woman and hail Rokoff and their companions to come to their rescue.

Fate smiled on them, for the gunfire had distracted Jane from her intention to keep a close eye on her unwilling assistants. She ran to the bow of the *Kincaid* to look for the source of the noise.

Seeing her off her guard, the two sailors crept stealthily toward her from behind.

The scraping on the deck of one sailor's shoes startled Jane to awareness of her danger—but too late. As she turned, both men leaped on her and knocked her to the deck. As she went down beneath them, she saw, outlined against the lesser gloom of the ocean, the figure of another man clamber onto the deck.

After all her pains, her heroic struggle for freedom had failed. With a stifled sob she gave up the unequal battle.

17

On the Deck of the *Kincaid*

When Mugambi had taken the pack back into the jungle, his goal was to find a dugout to transport the beasts of Tarzan to the side of the *Kincaid*. This was his homeland, of course, and he knew a likely spot not far upriver, along a small tributary of the Ugambi.

He arrived with the animals just at dusk, and found that his hunch had been good: he came across a canoe tied to the bank. Mugambi piled the apes and Sheeta into the craft in a hurry, and shoved out into the stream. It happened so quickly in the dusk that he had not noticed a huddled figure sleeping in the bottom.

No sooner were they afloat than a savage growling from one of the apes ahead of him in the dugout got Mugambi's attention. He looked down to see a cowering figure, trembling between him and the great ape. To his astonishment, it was a young African woman.

Mugambi's first priority was to command the ape not to attack her, and this he was able to communicate. He then turned to the woman and spoke in the dialect shared by the Mosula.

"I am sorry we took your canoe, but we have a very urgent errand to help my friend. I will not let these creatures harm you. I am Mugambi, chief of the Wagambi and friend of Tarzan of the Apes."

"My name is Afya, of the Mosula," she replied. "How can you be sure they will not harm us?"

"Because they obey me," smiled Mugambi. "I must hurry, but if you wish, I will put you ashore."

"No!" exclaimed Afya. "I do not want to go back. I was ordered to marry a hateful old man, and I fled. When I found this canoe, I decided to hide here for the night."

"Well, if you stay, you are risking your life. I can protect you from the apes, but when we reach our destination, there will probably be a battle with the enemies of my friend. They are surely as wicked as the old man you mentioned."

"Even so, I will stay," replied Afya.

At this, Mugambi set the apes to paddling and off they sped through darkness toward the Ugambi and the *Kincaid*. Before long, Mugambi could just make out the shadowy form of the steamer against the ocean horizon. He steered toward it, but strangely, it seemed to be moving away from him. He was about to urge the apes to paddle harder when suddenly, not three yards from the bow of his canoe, the outline of another dugout burst into view.

This new arrival's occupants spotted Mugambi's canoe at the same time, but they did not know who—or what—was onboard. A man in the bow called out a challenge just as the two dugouts were about to touch.

For an answer came the menacing growl of a panther, and the fellow found himself gazing into the flaming eyes of Sheeta, ready to leap.

Rokoff instantly realized his peril, and gave a quick command to open fire. Rifles cracked, and Afya screamed in terror—the sounds Jane had heard.

Tarzan of the Apes likewise heard them.

Before the clumsy paddlers in Mugambi's canoe could board their enemy, Rokoff had his canoe moving swiftly downstream. His crew paddled for their lives in the direction of the now-visible *Kincaid*.

After the vessel had come loose from the midstream shallows, it had swung into a slow eddy that returns upstream near the southern shore of the Ugambi, then circles back seaward about a hundred yards up. On this upstream current, the *Kincaid* was returning Jane Clayton directly toward the hands of her enemies.

When Tarzan sprang into the river, he could not see the vessel or the canoes. In the darkness, his only guide was the noise coming from the canoes. As he swam, he vividly remembered his last swim in the Ugambi, and a sudden shudder shook his giant frame. Twice he felt something brush his legs from the slimy depths below him, but nothing seized him.

Then he saw a dark mass loom suddenly before him where he had expected to find only open river, and he quite forgot about crocodiles.

It was so close that a few strokes brought him up to the thing. To his amazement his outstretched hand came in contact with a ship's side. He was in luck, for the rope ladder was at hand. As the agile ape-man scrambled over the vessel's rail, he heard the sounds of a struggle across the deck. He moved swiftly toward them.

The moon had risen now. Though the sky was still cloudy, the night was no longer quite as dark. He recognized where he was: the deck of the *Kincaid*. His keen eyes now also saw the figures of two men grappling with a woman.

He could not know who she was, though he suspected that it was the woman who had gone ashore with Anderssen. In any case, there was a woman fighting with two ruffians. Tarzan of the Apes had never, in his entire adult life, needed any greater excuse for action.

The first that either of the sailors knew that there was a new force at work on the ship was the clamp of a mighty hand on the backs of both necks. As if grabbed by heavy machinery, they were jerked suddenly from their prey.

"What means this?" growled a low voice in their ears.

They were given no time to reply. At the sound of that voice the young woman had sprung to her feet. She leaped toward their assailant with a little cry of joy:

"Tarzan!"

The ape-man hurled the two sailors across the deck, slamming them into the rail on the opposite side. There they lay stunned and terrified. Incredulity in his eyes, Tarzan gathered the woman into his arms.

There was not much time to celebrate their reunion.

As they recognized one another, the clouds parted. The new moonlight revealed half a dozen men coming aboard, led by Rokoff. There was enough visibility for him to see that the man before him was Lord Greystoke. He screamed in hysteria: "Fire, you idiots! Fire!"

Tarzan pushed Jane behind the cabin near which they had been standing and bounded quickly for Rokoff. Two of the men behind the Russian raised their rifles and fired at the charging ape-man.

Those behind the two who fired had other problems. A terrifying crew was boiling up the ladder and over the side.

First came five snarling apes, huge, manlike beasts with bared fangs and slavering jaws. Then came a giant African warrior, the tip of his long spear gleaming in the moonlight.

Behind him scrambled another creature, most fearsome of them all—Sheeta, the panther, with gleaming jaws agape and fiery eyes blazing in hate and blood lust.

The shots missed Tarzan, and he would have been on Rokoff in another instant had the great coward not dodged backward between his two henchmen and bolted screaming for the main cabin.

For the moment Tarzan was too busy with the two men in front of him to pursue the Russian. Battle raged around him as the apes, the panther, and Mugambi fought the rest of the Russian's party.

It did not last long. Against the great fangs of the apes of Akut, the tearing talons of Sheeta, and the deft spear-thrusts of Mugambi, only four survived to make a dash for the cabin, hoping to barricade themselves against further assault.

Here they found Rokoff. His desertion of them in combat was the last straw after months of brutal treatment. They had come to hate him, and it was time for some revenge.

Rokoff, true to form, groveled for his life. His abused subordinates paid no attention to his pleas. They threw him back out onto the deck as one cried:

"Go an' beg *them* for yer mercy, ye scurvy lubber!"

Tarzan saw Rokoff tumble from the cabin— but another saw him at the same moment.

It was Sheeta. With grinning jaws the mighty beast padded toward the terror-stricken man.

When Rokoff saw what stalked him, he stood paralyzed with fear, unable to do anything but shriek for salvation from the hideous death creeping toward him.

Tarzan took a step toward the Russian, his brain burning with a raging fire of vengeance. At last he had the murderer of his son at his mercy. The right to avenge was his.

Once in the past, Jane had dissuaded him from taking the law into his own hands and meting out to Rokoff the death he had so long deserved. This time, no one and nothing would stop him.

Before starting toward the trembling Russian, Tarzan had been a man. Now he was a beast of prey.

When he saw that Sheeta was about to rob him of his rightful justice, he called sharply to the panther.

The words seemed to break the spell of fear freezing the Russian in place. With a scream he turned and fled toward the bridge. After him pounced Sheeta, ignoring his master's warning voice.

Tarzan was about to leap after the two when he felt a light touch on his arm. Turning, he found Jane at his elbow.

"Do not leave me," she whispered, glancing about. "I am afraid."

Tarzan looked behind her, and he understood. All around were the hideous apes of Akut, with Mugambi ordering them back in tones accustomed to command. Even so, they were baring fangs and giving their low guttural warning barks. Were it not for the tall African, she might have already been harmed.

The ape-man sharply reinforced Mugambi's orders. He had forgotten for the moment that these were only beasts, unable to distinguish his friends from his foes. The battle had roused their savage natures as it had his own, and now all flesh outside the pack meant one thing: meat.

Tarzan turned again toward the Russian, frustrated that he might lose the pleasure of personal revenge on Rokoff—unless his archenemy managed to escape Sheeta. There was no hope of that, he saw, for his despised enemy had retreated to the end of the bridge. There he trembled, eyes wide, facing the sleek beast that slunk toward him.

There was no escape in the direction of the deck, unless he wanted a confrontation with Akut's apes. In fact, even now one of them was leaping the bridge rail to get at him. Rokoff stood as though petrified, his eyes protruding from their sockets, the cold sweat of terror clammy on his brow.

Rokoff could not move. His knees trembled. His voice broke in inarticulate shrieks of Russian, cries to a God whose commandments he had long disregarded.

With a last piercing wail he sank to his knees, and Sheeta sprang.

Full upon the man's breast the powerful body hurtled, tumbling the Russian to his back.

As the great fangs tore at the throat and chest, Jane Clayton turned away in horror; but not Tarzan of the Apes. A cold smile of satisfaction touched his lips. The scarlet scar on his forehead faded to the normal tan of his skin. Mugambi thumped the end of his great spear on the deck in triumph as he, too, watched Rokoff's final moments unfold.

Rokoff tried to fight against the growling, rending fate that had overtaken him, but it was hopeless. For all his countless crimes he was punished at last in this, the brief moment of his hideous death.

After his struggles ceased, Jane asked that Tarzan take the body from the panther and give what remained of Rokoff a decent human burial. Sheeta was not willing. The great cat rose snarling above its kill, threatening even the master it loved in its savage way. A dignified send-off for his wicked enemy was certainly not worth killing a friend over, and Tarzan let it be.

All that night Sheeta, the panther, crouched on the grisly thing that had been Nikolai Rokoff. The bridge of the *Kincaid* was slippery with blood. Beneath the brilliant tropic moon the great beast feasted.

When the sun rose the following morning, only gnawed and broken bones remained of Tarzan's great enemy.

Of the Russian's party, all were accounted for except Paulvitch. Four were prisoners in the *Kincaid's* main cabin; the rest were dead. Mugambi had called down to Afya just after Rokoff's death to tell her it was safe to come aboard, and soon the young woman stood on the deck of the steamer. Jane smiled a welcome, and Afya made her tribe's gesture of friendship in reply. Even without a common language, the eyes and manner of the two women communicated nearly as well as speech.

Tarzan ordered the men to get the engines going. One of the survivors was the mate. With the help of his knowledge, the ape-man planned to set a course for Jungle Island; but the morning brought a fierce gale from the west. The mate did not think it wise to risk the heavy seas, so all that day the ship lay sheltered in the river-mouth. The wind lessened by nightfall, but the shallows of the channel were treacherous enough by day, and Tarzan agreed to wait for morning.

The pack wandered the decks without hindrance by day, for they had soon learned through Tarzan and Mugambi that they must harm no one aboard the *Kincaid*; but at night they were confined below.

To his immense joy, Tarzan learned from Jane

that the little child who had died in the village of M'ganwazam was not their son. Who the baby could have been, or what had become of little Jack, they had no idea; with both Rokoff and Paulvitch gone, there was no way to find out.

At least there was still hope, for their baby son had obviously not been brought aboard the steamer. They had Anderssen's assurances that the little one he had brought to Jane's cabin had been the only baby on the *Kincaid* since she lay at dock in England, and there was no reason to doubt the words of the Swede.

18

Paulvitch Plots Revenge

As Jane and Tarzan stood on deck sharing their many adventures since they parted in London, a hidden watcher glared at them from the shore.

Plan after plan turned over in the vindictive brain of Alexei Paulvitch; he must somehow prevent the escape of the hated Englishman and his wife, and get revenge. But every plan he could come up with was either impossible or too merciful. His criminal mind was too twisted, of course, to realize that he and Rokoff had been the cause of their own miseries; he blamed them all on Tarzan.

In any case, he could accomplish nothing with half the Ugambi between him and the objects of his hatred. But how to get across the crocodile-infested waters? There was no canoe nearer than the Mosula village, and Paulvitch was not sure that the *Kincaid* would still be there when he got back. Yet it was his only chance. With a parting scowl at the two figures on deck, Paulvitch turned away to hasten through the dense thicket. The desire for revenge burned so hot within him that he forgot even his terror of the jungle's many dangers.

As the Russian stumbled on toward the Mosula village, a workable plan occurred to him.

He would come by night to the side of the *Kincaid*. Once onboard he would search out the surviving members of the ship's original crew and get them to mutiny against Tarzan and his beasts.

In his cabin were arms and ammunition and worse: hidden in a secret compartment in the cabin table was an infernal device. Back in Russia, he had been a member of the Nihilists, a radical group dedicated to the overthrow of the Tsar. They had believed him loyal to them, and had taught him a great deal about such devices. He had rewarded them by betraying them to the St. Petersburg police in return for gold and immunity. His treachery had sent several Nihilists to the gallows.

Yes, this device was just the thing, if he could get his hands on it. Within the little hardwood case was enough destructive power to wipe out every enemy onboard the steamer in less than a second. Paulvitch licked his lips in anticipation and urged his tired legs to greater speed.

All depended, of course, on the *Kincaid's* departure time. He must approach under cover of darkness. If he were sighted by Tarzan or Lady Greystoke, he would not get aboard.

He felt the gale blowing, and took heart, for it might keep the *Kincaid* from sailing. If it continued until nightfall, his odds would rise dramatically, for he knew how dangerous it was to try and navigate in the area of the river-mouth. Shallows and small islands were everywhere; they would surely wait for daylight.

It was well after noon when Paulvitch came to the Mosula village, where he found the people unfriendly and even hostile. Rokoff and Paulvitch always left a trail of suffering behind them, and the Mosula had been no exception.

Nonetheless, Paulvitch arrogantly demanded a canoe. The chief refused, summoned warriors, and ordered the Russian out of his village. The Russian looked around at the angry, muttering African spearmen, eager for any excuse to run him through. He might get one with his revolver, but it would be his final living act. Paulvitch had no choice but to leave, and a dozen of them escorted him to the edge of the clearing, warning him never to return.

Stifling his anger, Paulvitch slunk into the jungle. Once beyond the sight of the warriors, he paused and listened intently. He could hear the voices of his escort returning to the village. When he was sure that they were not following him, he wormed his way through the bushes to the edge of the river, still determined to somehow obtain a canoe. His life depended on his plan. Being abandoned here in the jungle—where the natives knew and despised him—was equivalent to a death sentence. The desperate Russian lay hidden in the brush, hoping for a small canoe to happen by.

He did not have long to wait before a small Mosula canoe came into sight. A young hunter was paddling lazily out into midstream from a point beside the village. When he reached the channel, he leaned back to relax, letting the sluggish current carry him along slowly.

The lad had no idea of the unseen enemy on the river's bank, moving downstream to keep pace with the canoe.

A mile below the village, the young African dipped his paddle into the water and forced his small canoe toward the bank. Paulvitch was elated: by pure luck, the youth had chosen to land on his side. The Russian headed for the spot where it seemed the canoe would touch the riverbank and hid there in the brush.

The young Mosula took his time pulling his canoe beneath the overhanging limb of a great tree, quite unaware of the Russian. Paulvitch avoided physical combat if at all possible, but now he measured his chances against the African youth. He had best use the revolver, he decided. There was just time enough to reach the *Kincaid* by nightfall; would the boy never finish fooling around? Paulvitch squirmed and fidgeted while the lad yawned and stretched. The young hunter examined the arrows in his quiver, tested his bow, and checked the edge of his hunting knife.

Again he yawned, glanced up at the riverbank, shrugged, and lay down in the bottom of his canoe for a little nap before going hunting.

Paulvitch half rose, muscles tensed, to glare down on his unsuspecting victim. The boy's lids closed. Presently, his chest rose and fell in the deep breaths of slumber. The time had come!

The Russian crept stealthily nearer. A branch rustled beneath his weight, and the lad stirred in his sleep. Paulvitch drew and leveled his revolver. For a moment it seemed that the youth would awaken, but he then relaxed again into deeper sleep.

Paulvitch crept closer. He could not afford to miss. He leaned close above the Mosula, bringing the revolver nearer and nearer until it stopped but a few inches above the innocent heart. The pressure of a finger lay between the harmless boy and eternity. There was a slight smile on the beardless lips of the boy.

Most people would have felt a pang of conscience to look on the handsome youth, but not Alexei Paulvitch. A sneer curled his bearded lip as his finger closed on the trigger.

There was a loud *boom*. A little hole appeared above the heart of the sleeping boy, about which lay a blackened rim of powder-burned flesh. The stricken youth sat up halfway, the smiling lips contorted by the nervous shock of sudden agony.

It was a short agony, for the young African warrior sank rapidly down into the canoe to his final rest. The killer dropped quickly into the boat beside the victim. Ruthless hands threw the dead boy overboard to a muddy, watery grave. The coveted canoe was in sole possession of a man far more savage than the youth whose life he had taken. Casting off the tie rope and seizing the paddle, Paulvitch soon had the canoe moving downstream toward the Ugambi at top speed.

Night had fallen by the time the bloodstained craft shot out into the current of the larger stream. Constantly the Russian strained his eyes into the increasing darkness ahead, hoping to see the *Kincaid* at anchor. The storm was easing. Was it still there, or had the ape-man decided it was safe to sail? For Paulvitch the future was uncertain, but one thing was quite sure: if the steamer turned out to be gone, his prospects were very poor.

In the darkness it seemed to the Russian that he was moving very quickly. He became convinced that the ship had left her moorings and that he had already passed her former point of anchor. Then he rounded a bend to see the flickering light from a ship's lantern.

Paulvitch nearly cried out in triumph. The *Kincaid* had not departed! Life and vengeance were to be his!

He stopped paddling the moment he spied the

gleaming beacon of hope ahead of him. Silently he drifted down the muddy waters of the Ugambi, occasionally dipping his paddle's blade in to better guide his canoe to the vessel's side.

As he approached more closely, the dark bulk of a ship loomed out of the inky night. No sound came from the vessel's deck. Paulvitch drifted unseen until he was close to the *Kincaid's* side. Only the momentary scraping of his canoe's nose against the ship's planking broke the silence of the night.

Trembling with nervous excitement, the Russian kept still for several minutes; but there was no sound from above to indicate that he had been discovered. Stealthily he worked his craft toward the *Kincaid's* bow until the ropes of the bowsprit were directly above him. He could just reach them. After tying his canoe to one of them, he raised himself quietly aloft.

A moment later he dropped softly to the deck. The thought of the beasts aboard this ship—as well as two fierce men—sent cold tremors up his cowardly spine, but his life depended on success here. He steeled himself against what might come.

No one was on watch. Paulvitch crept stealthily through the silence toward the main cabin. Raising the hatch, he saw one of the *Kincaid's* crew reading by the light of a smoky lantern.

Paulvitch knew the man well: a surly cut-throat, perfect for his purposes. Gently the Russian lowered himself through the hatch to the cabin ladder, keeping his eyes on the reading man, ready to warn him to silence. The sailor was so deeply immersed in his reading that the Russian reached the cabin floor unobserved. There he turned and whispered the reader's name.

The man raised his eyes, and they went wide for a moment as they recognized Rokoff's lieutenant, only to narrow instantly in a scowl of disapproval.

"The devil!" he exclaimed. "Where did you come from? We all thought you were done for, like you ought to have been a long time ago. His Lordship will be mighty pleased to see you."

Paulvitch crossed to the sailor's side with a warm smile on his lips, extending his hand as though the sailor were a long-lost friend. The sailor returned neither the hand nor the smile.

"I've come to help you," explained Paulvitch, "to get rid of the Englishman and his beasts. That way, when we get back to civilization, no one will put the law onto us. We can sneak in on the humans while they sleep—Greystoke, his wife, and that big African. Afterward it will be a simple matter to clean up the beasts. Where are they?"

"They're below," replied the sailor. "But just let me tell you something, Paulvitch. You haven't got no way to turn us against the Englishman. You two treated us like dogs, and we got no love for you. The other's dead, like you'll be before long."

"You're turning against me?" demanded Paulvitch.

The other nodded, and then after a momentary pause for thought, he smiled coldly.

"Unless," he said, "you can make it worth my while."

"You wouldn't make me go back to the jungle, would you?" asked Paulvitch. "Why, I'd die there in a week."

"You'd have a chance there," replied the sailor. "Here, you wouldn't have none. Why, if I woke up my maties here, they'd probably kill you before his Lordship had the chance. It's mighty lucky for you that I'm the one to be awake now."

"You're crazy," cried Paulvitch. "Don't you know that Greystoke will have you all hanged when he gets you back into the reach of the law?"

"No, he won't do nothing of the kind," replied the sailor. "He says that you and Rokoff was to blame for it all—the rest of us was just tools. See?"

For half an hour the Russian switched tactics as he tried all his persuasive skill. One minute he seemed near tears; in the next he would either be promising tremendous rewards or terrible punishment. The man was unmoved. Eventually, he made his position plain with an icy smile:

"Enough of all that, Russian. I give you two choices. I can turn you over to Lord Greystoke right now; or I can let you get loose, but it'll cost every penny on you, and everything in your cabin." He paused, then went on: "And make up your mind, because I want to turn in for the night. Come now, choose—his Lordship or the jungle?"

"You'll be sorry for this," grumbled the Russian.

"Shut up," ordered the sailor. "If you act up, maybe I'll just keep you here after all."

Paulvitch had no intention of falling into Tarzan's hands if he could avoid it. The jungle might be terrifying, but it was far preferable to the certain death he could expect from the ape-man.

"Is anyone sleeping in my cabin?" he asked.

The sailor shook his head. "No," he said. "Lord and Lady Greystoke have the captain's cabin. The mate is in his own, and there ain't no one in yours."

"I'll go and get my valuables for you," said Paulvitch.

"I'll go with you to make sure you don't try any funny business," said the sailor, and he followed the Russian up the ladder to the deck.

At the cabin entrance the sailor halted to keep watch, letting Paulvitch go alone to his cabin. He lit a lantern, then piled up his few belongings on the table. He searched his mind feverishly for some better plan, and remembered the little black box in the hidden compartment.

The Russian's face gleamed with wicked satisfaction as he felt beneath the tabletop. A moment later he pulled out what he sought. He opened the clasp of the small box to reveal two compartments. One was visible. It contained a clock-like mechanism and a small battery; wires ran from the clock and the battery into the other compartment. The second compartment was not visible, for it was covered and sealed with solidified tar. He then began to wind the clock, muffling the noise by throwing clothing over it. Paulvitch listened intently for any sound that might indicate someone coming in, but he was not interrupted. When he finished, he set a pointer on a small dial at the side of the clock, then closed and hid the box once again.

With a sinister smile on his bearded lips, he then gathered up his valuables, blew out the lamp, and stepped from his cabin to the side of the waiting sailor.

"Here are my things," said the Russian. "Now let me go."

"I'll first take a look in your pockets," replied the sailor. "You might have overlooked some thing that won't be of no use to you in the jungle, but that'll come in mighty handy to a poor sailorman in London. Ah! Just as I thought," he said an instant later as he withdrew a roll of money from Paulvitch's inside coat pocket.

The Russian scowled and swore, but argument was pointless. At least, he thought to himself, the sailor would never reach London to spend the money. Suppressing the temptation to taunt the man with a hint of the fate that soon awaited him and the whole ship's company, he crossed the deck and climbed down to his canoe in silence.

A minute or two later he was paddling toward the shore to be swallowed up in the darkness of the jungle night. Had he known what the long years ahead held for him, he would instead have fled to the certain death of the open sea.

After making sure Paulvitch was gone, the sailor returned to the main cabin, where he hid away his newly acquired goods and went to bed.

Meanwhile, in the Russian's former cabin, the clock ticked on toward his revenge on the hard-luck *Kincaid* and its unsuspecting sleepers.

19

The Last of the *Kincaid*

Shortly after daybreak Tarzan was on deck evaluating the weather. The wind had abated. The sky was cloudless. Every condition seemed ideal for the return voyage to Jungle Island, to drop off the beasts—then home!

The ape-man woke up the mate and instructed him to get the *Kincaid* under way at the earliest possible moment. The remaining members of the crew, trusting Lord Greystoke's promise of immunity from prosecution, went cheerfully to their duties.

Mugambi let the beasts out of the hold, and they wandered the deck at will. This made the crew and Afya very uneasy. They would not soon forget what the fangs and talons of these creatures had done in battle, and the pack looked eager for further prey. Under the watchful eyes of Tarzan and Mugambi, however, Sheeta and the apes of Akut were on good behavior. Even so, Afya kept close to

Mugambi, and the sailors avoided the beasts.

At last, the *Kincaid* slipped down the Ugambi and ran out on the shimmering waters of the Atlantic dawn. Tarzan and Jane Clayton watched the green African shoreline receding in the ship's wake. For once the ape-man left his native soil without a single pang of regret. No ship in the world could be swift enough to satisfy the urgency of his search for his lost son. The *Kincaid* was slow but made steady progress. In a little while, the low hills of Jungle Island came into view to the west.

In the former cabin of Alexei Paulvitch, the thing within the black box ticked on. Second by second, a little arm attached to one of its gears came nearer and nearer to another little arm which Paulvitch had set at a certain point on the dial beside the clockwork.

When those two arms touched, the ticking would cease forever.

Jane and Tarzan stood on the bridge looking out toward Jungle Island. The sailors were forward, getting ready for landfall. The beasts had gone to sleep in the shade of the galley. All was quiet and peaceful.

Suddenly a terrific explosion shook the vessel from stem to stern. The cabin roof shot up into the air. A cloud of dense smoke puffed far above the *Kincaid*.

Pandemonium broke loose. The apes of Akut, terrified by the sound, ran about snarling and growling. Sheeta leaped here and there, screaming out startled cries of terror that sent the ice of fear straight to the hearts of the *Kincaid's* crew.

Afya let out a shriek of fear and quickly put the other humans between her and the animals, shaking in fright. Only Tarzan, his wife, and Mugambi retained their composure. Scarcely had the debris settled than the ape-man and the African were among the beasts, speaking to them in soothing tones to assure them that the immediate danger was over.

It did not take long to see that their greatest danger now was fire. Flames were licking hungrily at the splintered wood of the wrecked cabin, and had already caught on the lower deck through a huge jagged hole blown by the explosion. By a miracle, none of the ship's company was hurt. The crew did not need orders; they rigged a pump and began to fight the fire.

The origin of the blast would forever remain a mystery to all but one onboard. The sailor who had let Paulvitch get away guessed at the truth, but kept his suspicion to himself. If the rest found out that he was guilty of letting Lord Greystoke's archenemy aboard where he might set up a bomb to blow them all to kingdom come, it would go hard with him.

The water that the sailors poured into the hole seemed to be spreading the blaze. It became apparent to Tarzan that the explosion had scattered something oily on the surrounding wood. The flames were gaining headway in spite of the efforts of the crew.

Fifteen minutes after the explosion, great black clouds of smoke began rising from the hold of the doomed vessel. The flames had reached the engine room, and the ship had stopped moving. Her fate was as certain as though the waters had already closed above her charred and smoking remains.

"It is useless to remain onboard," remarked the ape-man to the mate. "There may be other explosions. Since we cannot hope to save her, the safest thing is to take to the boats immediately and make land."

There was no alternative. The sailors were able to quickly gather what belongings they could carry, for the fire had not yet reached the main cabin. Two boats were swiftly lowered, and soon both were heading into the surf of Jungle Island. Eager and anxious, the beasts of Tarzan sniffed the familiar air of their native island. The boats had barely touched the sand when Sheeta and the apes of Akut were over the bows and racing swiftly toward the jungle. A half-sad smile curved the lips of the ape-man as he watched them go.

"Goodbye, my friends," he murmured. "You have been good and faithful allies, and I will miss you."

"They will return, will they not, dear?" asked Jane Clayton, at his side.

"They may and they may not," replied the ape-man. "They have never been comfortable near so many civilized human beings, such as you and the members of the crew. Mugambi and I affected them less, for he and I are, like them, native to the jungle. They would be less nervous around Afya as well, but they sense her fear as easily as they sense Mugambi's confidence. Perhaps my beasts feel that they cannot trust themselves near so much perfectly good food; they may worry that they will lose control and help themselves to a mouthful."

Jane laughed. "I think they are just trying to escape you," she teased, "and all your tedious restrictions. In their minds, you are always making them stop doing something for no good reason other than that you command it. They are like little children, eager to get away from boring discipline. If they come back, though, I hope they won't come by night."

"Or come hungry, eh?" laughed Tarzan.

For two hours after landing, the little party stood watching the *Kincaid* burn. Then came the faint sound of a second explosion, which the mate explained was the bursting of the boilers. Within a few minutes, the wrecked steamer sank beneath the waves.

The cause of the first explosion remained a mystery—and a subject of much speculation.

20

Jungle Island Again

The party first needed to locate fresh water and make camp. The mate doubted that the *Kincaid's* lifeboats could reach the mainland even in ideal conditions. They might be stuck on Jungle Island for months—maybe even years.

Tarzan led the party to the nearest source of water, and there the men began to construct shelters and basic furniture while Tarzan went hunting. He trusted Jane's safety to Mugambi and Afya, for he certainly could not leave her alone with the cutthroats that crewed the *Kincaid*.

Lady Greystoke suffered most of all, for her anguish over her son made the hardships of their current situation seem trivial. Now she might never learn of her first-born's fate, much less be able to help him, and she imagined the worst.

A visit to the beach the next morning brought awful news: the boats from the *Kincaid* had been washed out to sea, most likely by a combination of high winds and tide. Now they were truly stranded.

For the next two weeks, each member of the party went about his or her assigned duties. A daylight watch was maintained on a bluff near the camp overlooking the sea. A huge pile of dry branches was gathered nearby to use for a signal fire, and they had attached the mate's red undershirt to a tall makeshift pole set into the ground. The vigil was a fruitless one, for the sea's surface remained empty.

Tarzan finally suggested that they attempt to build a vessel to return to the mainland. Both he and Mugambi knew how to make basic tools, and at first the men turned eagerly to the work. But as time went on and the task began to loom larger, they fell to grumbling and quarreling among themselves. Eventually the men neglected their work, going off into the jungle by twos to loaf, explore, and hunt.

Akut's apes and Sheeta never came within sight of camp, though Tarzan sometimes met them in the jungle as he hunted.

And as matters went from bad to worse in the castaways' camp on the east coast of Jungle Island, another camp came into being on the north coast.

Here in a little cove lay the small schooner *Cowrie*. A few days earlier the *Cowrie's* decks had run red with the blood of her officers and the loyal members of her crew. The schooner had had the misfortune to have such men as Gust, Momulla the Maori, and that archfiend Kai Shang of Fachan as part of the crew. There were ten other scum of the South Sea ports in camp, but those three were the brains; they had led the mutiny. Their goal had been to seize the catch of pearls that were the *Cowrie's* immensely valuable cargo.

It was Kai Shang who had murdered the captain in his sleep. Momulla the Maori had led the attack on the officer of the watch. Gust, a Swede, had quietly kept clear of the fighting—not because he had scruples about killing, but because he was unwilling to risk his own skin. But with the mutiny over, Gust felt he should be their leader. He had even gone so far as to begin wearing the murdered captain's clothing. He liked the clothing because of the appearance of seafaring authority that its decoration gave him.

Kai Shang was annoyed. He had no love for authority, and he had no intention of taking orders from an ordinary Swedish sailor. Momulla, a proud Maori warrior from New Zealand, liked people who were in authority even less than Kai Shang did.

The seeds of discontent were, therefore, already planted in the mutineers' camp at the north edge of Jungle Island. But Kai Shang realized that he must act carefully. Gust alone knew how to navigate them to the Indian Ocean, where they could sell their ill-gotten wealth with no questions asked.

The day before they spotted the sheltered harbor, the man on watch had seen the smoke and funnels of a warship on the southern horizon. None of them wanted to be investigated by a man-of-war, so they had decided to hide for a few days. Gust did not want to venture out to sea again; he insisted that the ship was likely searching for them. Kai Shang disagreed, on the grounds that only the mutineers knew what had happened aboard the *Cowrie*, but Gust was unconvinced. More significantly, his selfish mind had brewed up a scheme that would double his share of the pearls. Since only he could navigate the schooner, the others could not leave Jungle Island without him. Why not take perhaps half the crew—just enough to man the *Cowrie*—and leave Kai Shang, Momulla, and the rest of the crew to fend for themselves?

It would have been far more comfortable for the entire party to remain onboard the ship while they hid in the harbor. However, because of their mistrust of one another, it had been mutually decided that they would camp ashore. Each suspected the others of enough treachery that not more than two or three men were allowed on shipboard at once unless the entire company was present.

Gust waited patiently for the moment when Kai Shang, Momulla, and three or four of the others would be out exploring or hunting. The Swede racked his brain for some way to bring this about; the only solution he could devise was to organize many hunting parties. But the Kai Shang suspected something, for he would never go hunting unless Gust himself went.

One day, in secret, Kai Shang told Momulla the Maori of his growing suspicions about the Swede. He had no outright evidence, but he had a mind as evil as that of Gust. Kai Shang knew what he himself would be trying to do if he had Gust's knowledge of seamanship.

Momulla wanted to go immediately and run a long knife through the traitor's heart. Kai Shang disagreed; they needed the Swede alive to get to their destination. After some discussion, they decided to try to frighten Gust into cooperating with them. With this in mind, the Maori went to talk with the self-appointed "captain" of the party.

When Momulla suggested immediate departure, Gust raised again the familiar objection regarding the prowling warship. The New Zealand tribesman scoffed, pointing out the flaw in this view: no one aboard any warship had any reason to even suspect a mutiny, much less be hunting mutineers.

"Ah!" exclaimed Gust; "there is where you are wrong. You are lucky to have a civilized man like me to tell you what to do. You are an ignorant savage, Momulla, who knows nothing of wireless."

The Maori leaped to his feet and laid his hand on the hilt of his knife.

"I am no savage," he shouted.

"I was only joking," the Swede hastened to explain. "We are old friends, Momulla; we cannot afford to quarrel, at least not while old Kai Shang is plotting to steal all the pearls from us. If he could find a man to navigate the *Cowrie* he would leave us in a minute. All his talk about getting away from here is just a distraction while he figures out some way to get rid of us."

"But what has the wireless to do with our remaining here?" asked Momulla.

"Oh yes," replied Gust, scratching his head, wondering if the Maori could be so ignorant as to believe the gigantic lie he was about to tell. "Oh yes! You see, every warship has a gadget called a "wireless." It lets them talk to other ships hundreds of miles away, and it lets them listen to all that is said on these other ships. When you fellows were taking the *Cowrie*, you made a whole lot of noise, including plenty of loud talking. No doubt that warship was a-lying off south of us listening to it all. Of course, they might not have learned the name of the ship, but they heard enough to know that the crew of some ship was mutinying against her officers. So you see, they'll search every ship they sight for a long time to come, and they may not be far away now." Gust assumed an air of calm confidence.

Momulla sat eyeing Gust for some time in silence. At last he rose.

"I have known many liars, and you are the

biggest liar of all," he said. "If you don't get us on our way by tomorrow, you'll never have another chance to lie. I heard two of the men saying that they'd like to run a knife into you, and that if you kept them in this hole any longer they'd do it."

"Go and ask Kai Shang about the wireless," replied Gust. "He will tell you that it exists, and that vessels can talk to one another across many miles of water. Then tell the two men who wish to kill me that if they do so, they will never get to spend their share of the loot. Only I can get you safely to any port."

So Momulla went to Kai Shang and asked him: was there such a thing as a wireless? Could ships really talk with each other at great distances? Kai Shang told him that there was, and they could.

Momulla was puzzled; but still he wished to leave the island and was willing to take his chances on the open sea rather than remain here any longer.

"If we only had someone else who could navigate a ship!" wailed Kai Shang.

That afternoon Momulla went hunting with two other Maoris. They hunted toward the south, and had not gone far from camp when they were surprised by the sound of voices ahead of them in the jungle.

None of their own men had gone in this direction. Because they had no idea there were other humans on the island, they began to suspect that it might be haunted—possibly by the ghosts of the murdered officers and men of the *Cowrie*. Panic began to set in.

But Momulla was more curious than superstitious. Motioning his companions to follow his example, he made his people's gesture of apology and friendship toward whatever ghosts of their victims might be lurking out there. After this, he led his nervous crew cautiously forward toward the voices.

Before long, they were relieved to see two flesh-and-blood men sitting on a fallen log, having a discussion. Momulla halted his companions so they would not be seen by the strangers. Then he listened.

One of the men on the log was Schneider, mate of the *Kincaid*, and the other was a seaman named Schmidt.

"I think we can do it, Schmidt," Schneider was saying. "A good canoe wouldn't be hard to build, and three of us could paddle it to the mainland in a day if the weather is decent. There ain't no use waiting for the men to build a big enough boat to take the whole party, for they're sick of working like slaves all day long. It ain't none of our business anyway to save the Englishman. Let him look out for himself, says I." He paused for a moment, then continued, watching Schmidt's reaction carefully: "But we might take the white woman. It would be a shame to leave a nice-lookin' lady like her in such a God-forsaken place as this here island."

Schmidt looked up and grinned. "Why didn't you say so in the first place? And what's in it for me if I help you?"

"She ought to pay us well to get her back to civilization," explained Schneider. "An' I tell you what I'll do. I'll divide that money with the two men that helps me. I'll take half an' you an' whoever else can divide the other half. I just want off this island. What do you say?"

"Suits me," replied Schmidt. "I wouldn't know how to reach the mainland myself, an' neither does any o' the other fellows, so it's you I've got to stick with."

Momulla the Maori pricked up his ears. He knew a little bit of nearly every language spoken on the seas, and had sailed on enough English ships to understand most of the plotters' dialogue. He rose to his feet and stepped into the clearing. Schneider and his companion were startled, and Schneider reached for his revolver. Momulla raised his right hand, palm forward, as a sign of peaceful intent.

"I am a friend," he said. "I heard you, but I will keep your secret. We can help each other," he told Schneider. "You can navigate a ship, but you have no ship. We have a ship, but no one to navigate it. Here is my plan: you come with us, and ask no questions. After you have landed us at a certain port, which we will name for you later, you may take the ship and the woman wherever you like, and we will ask no questions. Is it a bargain?"

Schneider wanted more information, and got as much as Momulla thought was safe to give him. Then the Maori suggested that they speak with Kai Shang. The two members of the *Kincaid's* company followed Momulla and his fellows to a point in the jungle near the mutineers' camp. Momulla told the two newcomers to stay there while he brought Kai Shang. Then, in the Maori language, he ordered his shipmates to stand guard in order to make sure the two did not change their minds and attempt to escape. Schneider and Schmidt did not know it, but they were practically prisoners.

Momulla found Kai Shang and quietly told him of their good fortune. The two ringleaders returned to the edge of camp. Speaking with Schneider, Kai Shang determined that while Schneider was probably not telling him the whole truth, he was a fellow rogue anxious to leave the island. In that case, he could be trusted far enough for Kai Shang's purposes—and onboard the *Cowrie*, if Schneider failed to cooperate, he could be forced to.

When Schneider and Schmidt left to return to their own camp, it was with great relief. At last they had a reasonable plan for leaving the island on a seaworthy craft. There would be no more hard labor at shipbuilding and no need to risk their lives on a crudely built makeshift canoe with an even chance of sinking.

Also, they would have help in capturing the

woman—or rather, women, for when Momulla had learned that there was a black woman in the other camp he had insisted that she too be brought along.

As Kai Shang and Momulla entered their camp, both realized that they no longer needed Gust. There was no reason to risk his treachery for even another hour. They marched directly toward Gust's tent.

The Maori felt the edge of his long knife with one grimy, callused thumb. At that moment Gust was in the cook's tent, only a few feet from his own. He heard the approach of Kai Shang and Momulla but did not dream that it might mean anything.

Luck was on Gust's side, for he happened to glance out of the cook's tent at the very moment that Kai Shang and Momulla approached the entrance to his, and the stealth of their movements suggested ill intentions. Then, just as they slunk inside, Gust caught a glimpse of the long knife behind Momulla's back.

The Swede's eyes opened wide, his skin paled, and he felt the hair prickle on his neck. He ducked quickly out of the cook's tent. He might have delusions of power, but he was not a fool: they had obviously come to murder him. If so, his ability to navigate no longer assured his safety. Something must have happened to make it worth their while to eliminate him.

Without a pause Gust darted across the beach and into the jungle. He feared the jungle with its strange noises and tangled mazes, but he feared Kai Shang and Momulla far more. The dangers of the jungle were beyond his control, but the danger from his companions was quite clear—cold steel or a rope. He had seen Kai Shang strangle a man at Pai-sha in a dark alleyway back of Loo Kotai's place. He feared the rope, therefore, more than he did the knife of the Maori.

The jungle had far more pity than either of those men.

21

The Law of the Jungle

By combining threats with promises of reward, the ape-man had gotten enough work out of the sailors to have nearly finished the hull of a large skiff. He and Mugambi had ultimately done much of the work themselves, even while doing all the camp's hunting.

Schneider had been grumbling a lot; now he quit the work entirely and went off into the jungle with Schmidt to hunt. Rather than add to the tension in camp, Tarzan had just let them go. The next day, however, Schneider seemed to regret his action, and he and Schmidt got cheerfully back to work.

Lord Greystoke congratulated himself that the men had come to their senses. About noon, buoyed by a sense of general relief, he set out in search of a herd of deer Schneider had reported seeing. Off he swung toward the southwest, moving easily through the tangled forest.

As he disappeared into the trees, half a dozen

men were moving stealthily through the jungle toward the camp from the north. They believed themselves to be unobserved, but they were wrong; the tall Swede had trailed them since they left camp. In Gust's eyes were hate, fear, and curiosity: where were Kai Shang and Momulla so quietly going? What did they expect to find? He would follow them and find out, and if he could thwart their plans, so much the better.

At first he had thought they were hunting him, but soon he realized that this made no sense. Driving him out of camp had accomplished their goal. Neither Kai Shang nor Momulla would bother to hunt him down unless it would somehow enrich them. Gust had no money. They must be searching for someone else. Who that someone might be, though, the Swede had no idea.

Presently the mutineers came to a halt and hid in the foliage along the game trail. To better observe, Gust clambered into the branches of a tree to the rear of them.

Before long, a strange white man came in sight from the south, moving cautiously.

At sight of the newcomer, Momulla and Kai Shang broke cover and greeted him. Gust could not overhear the discussion. After some time had passed, the man returned the way he had come.

It was Schneider. As he neared his camp, he circled to the opposite side, then ran breathlessly in. He hastened excitedly to Mugambi.

"Quick!" he cried. "Those apes of yours have caught Schmidt and will kill him if we do not hurry! You alone can call them off. Take Jones and Sullivan—you may need help—and get to him as quick as you can. Follow the game trail south for about a mile. I am too tired to keep up with you." Then the *Kincaid's* mate threw himself on the ground, panting realistically.

Mugambi hesitated, for his first duty was to guard the two women. While he considered what to do, Jane Clayton, who had heard Schneider's story, added her pleas to those of the mate.

"Do not delay," she urged. "We will be all right here. Mr. Schneider will remain with us. Go, Mugambi. The poor fellow must be saved."

Schmidt grinned in his hiding place in a bush at the edge of the camp. Mugambi doubted the wisdom of leaving, but Jane's encouragement convinced him. He started southward, with Jones and Sullivan at his heels.

No sooner had Mugambi disappeared than Schmidt rose and darted north into the jungle. A few minutes later the face of Kai Shang of Fachan appeared at the edge of the clearing. Schneider motioned to him that the coast was clear.

Jane Clayton and Afya were sitting at the opening of Jane's tent, their backs toward the approaching ruffians. Neither had any idea of strangers in camp until a half-dozen ragged villains suddenly appeared about them.

"Come!" said Kai Shang, motioning the women to arise and follow him.

Jane Clayton sprang to her feet and looked around for Schneider, only to see him standing behind the newcomers, grinning. At his side stood Schmidt. Clearly she and Afya were the victims of a plot.

"What is the meaning of this?" she asked Schneider.

"It means that we have found a ship and that we can now escape from Jungle Island," he replied.

"Why did you send Mugambi and the others into the jungle?" she inquired.

"They are not coming with us—only you and I and the African woman."

"Come!" repeated Kai Shang, and seized Jane Clayton's wrist.

One of the Maoris grasped Afya by the arm. When she began to protest, he struck her across the mouth.

Mugambi raced south through the jungle, with Jones and Sullivan trailing far behind. For a mile he continued in search of Schmidt, but he saw no signs of the missing man or of any of Akut's apes. He began to be suspicious. At last he halted and gave the strange call that he and Tarzan used to hail the great apes.

There was no response. Jones and Sullivan caught up with the black warrior as he stood voicing his summons. For another half-mile the

African searched, calling occasionally.

Finally, the truth flashed on him. With the speed of a frightened deer, he wheeled and dashed back toward camp. When he arrived, his worst fears were confirmed: Lady Greystoke and Afya were gone. So was Schneider.

When Jones and Sullivan joined Mugambi, his first furious impulse was to kill them as conspirators in the plot. They saved their lives by convincing him—at least partially—that they had known nothing of it.

As they stood trying to figure out where the women had been taken and Schneider's reason for kidnapping them, Tarzan of the Apes swung from the branches of a tree and crossed the clearing toward them.

He realized immediately that something was very wrong, and when he had heard Mugambi's story, his teeth ground angrily together as he frowned in thought. For Schneider to just kidnap Jane Clayton, on a small island where he knew he could never escape Tarzan's vengeance, was greater foolishness than Schneider seemed capable of. Then it dawned on him.

Schneider must have found a way to get off Jungle Island with his prisoners. But why take Afya as well? He had never shown any interest in her before this. Perhaps someone else had. There must be others, one of whom had wanted the African woman.

"Come," said Tarzan, "the only thing to do now is to follow the trail."

As he finished speaking, a tall, unfamiliar figure emerged from the jungle and came straight toward them. Not one of them had dreamed that there were any other people on Jungle Island. It was Gust, and he came directly to the point.

"Your women were stolen," he said. "If you want ever to see them again, follow me. If we do not hurry, the *Cowrie* will soon be out to sea."

"Who are you?" asked Tarzan. "What do you know of the theft of my wife and Afya?"

"I heard Kai Shang and Momulla the Maori plot with a man from your camp. They meant to kill me, and I fled from our camp. Now I will get even with them. Come!"

Gust led the four men of Tarzan's camp at a rapid trot through the jungle toward the north. Would they arrive in time?

When the little party finally broke through the last of the foliage, and the harbor and the ocean lay before them, they realized that fate had been cruel. The *Cowrie* was already under sail and moving slowly out of the harbor.

What were they to do? It seemed the final blow. If ever in all his life Tarzan of the Apes had reason to abandon hope, it was now. He watched helplessly as the ship bearing his wife to some frightful fate moved gracefully over the rippling water, so very near and yet so hideously far away.

He stood watching the vessel in silence. He saw it turn toward the east and finally disappear around a headland, destination unknown. Then he dropped on his haunches and buried his face in his hands.

It was after dark when the five men returned to the camp on the east shore. The night was hot and sultry. No breeze disturbed the foliage or the mirror-like surface of the ocean. Only a gentle swell rolled softly in on the beach.

Never had Tarzan seen the great Atlantic so ominously at peace. He was gazing sadly out to sea toward the mainland, feeling hopeless, when from the jungle close behind the camp came the uncanny wail of a panther.

There was a familiar note in the weird cry, and by reflex Tarzan turned his head and answered. A moment later the sleek figure of Sheeta slunk out onto the beach lit only by the brilliant stars of a clear, moonless night. He came silently to Tarzan's side.

It had been long since Tarzan had seen his old comrade, but the soft purr assured him that the animal still recalled their old bond. The ape-man petted and fondled the savage head while his eyes continued to search the blackness of the waters.

Presently he started. What was that?

He strained his eyes into the night. Then he turned and called aloud to the men resting in their tents. They came running to his side, though Gust hesitated when he saw Tarzan's companion.

"Look!" cried Tarzan. "A light! A ship's light!

It must be the *Cowrie*. They are becalmed." And then with renewed hope: "We can reach them! The skiff will carry us easily."

"They are well armed," Gust warned. "Just five of us could not take the ship."

"There are six now," replied Tarzan, pointing to Sheeta, "and we can have more still in a half-hour. Sheeta is the equivalent of twenty men, and the few others I can bring will add the equivalent of a hundred to our fighting strength. You do not know them."

The ape-man turned and raised his head toward the jungle, and from his lips bellowed again and again the fearsome summons of the bull-ape.

Presently from the jungle came an answering cry, then more. Gust shuddered. Whom—or what—had he fallen in with? Kai Shang and Momulla started to seem far less frightening than a great white giant who could command panthers and other unknown beasts, all accompanied by a big, fierce-looking African warrior.

In a few minutes the apes of Akut came crashing through the underbrush. Meanwhile, the five men had been struggling with the clumsy bulk of the skiff's hull, and now they had it at the water's edge. The oars from the two lost small boats of the *Kincaid* had been in use as makeshift tent poles, and they were hastily brought. By the time Akut and his followers came down to the water, the party was ready to embark.

Once again the fierce crew entered Tarzan's service, taking up their places in the skiff unquestioningly. The four men—for Gust absolutely refused to come—began to paddle, and some of the apes followed their example. Presently the skiff was moving quietly out to sea in the direction of the bobbing light.

A sleepy sailor kept a lazy watch on the *Cowrie's* deck, while in the cabin below Schneider paced up and down, arguing with Jane Clayton. She had been locked in the cabin but had found a revolver in a table drawer; now she had it aimed at the traitor. Afya stayed behind her as Schneider threatened and pleaded and argued. Jane was unmoved.

Suddenly, from the deck above came a shout of warning and a gunshot. For an instant Jane Clayton relaxed her vigilance by looking up toward the cabin skylight. Immediately, Schneider was on her.

The first that the watching mutineer on deck knew of any other craft in the area was when the head and shoulders of a man poked over the ship's side. Instantly, the fellow sprang to his feet with a cry, leveled his revolver at the intruder, and fired. These were the sounds that had distracted Jane.

Soon the imagined security of the deck gave way to deadly chaos. The crew of the *Cowrie* rushed from the main cabin, armed with revolvers, cutlasses, and long knives; but the alarm had come too late. Already the beasts of Tarzan were on the ship's deck, with Tarzan, Mugambi, and the *Kincaid's* two crewmen.

The sight of the frightful beasts was too much for the mutineers. Those who had revolvers fired a few shots, and they all ran for safety.

Some took to the rigging, which was a fatal mistake given the normal mode of travel of the apes. Screaming with terror, the Maoris were dragged from their lofty perches. Tarzan had gone to look for Jane, and so was not present to control the pack. Still infuriated at having been deceived, Mugambi grimly chose to let the beasts do as they liked.

Sheeta, in the meanwhile, had sunk his great fangs into but a single jugular. For a moment he mauled the corpse of the sailor. Then he spied Kai Shang darting down the companionway toward his cabin.

With a shrill scream Sheeta was after him, and the terrified man let forth a desperate cry. But Kai Shang reached his cabin a fraction of a second ahead of the panther, leaped in, and slammed the door behind him—just too late. Sheeta's great body hurtled against it before the catch engaged, and a moment later Kai Shang was shrieking in the back of the upper bunk.

Lightly, Sheeta sprang after his victim. A moment later the wicked days of Kai Shang of Fachan ended with Sheeta gorging himself on tough, stringy flesh.

Schneider had just wrenched the revolver away from Jane when the cabin door opened. A tall, half-naked white man leaped instantly across the cabin onto the traitor's back.

Schneider felt sinewy fingers at his throat. He turned his head to see who had attacked him, and his eyes went wide when he saw the face of the ape-man close above his own.

Tarzan's fingers tightened on the mate's throat. He tried to scream, to plead, but no sound came forth. His eyes protruded as he struggled for freedom, for breath, for life.

Jane Clayton seized her husband's hands and tried to drag them from the throat of the dying man; but Tarzan only shook his head.

"Not again," he said quietly. "When I have spared scoundrels, my mercy has been rewarded by suffering for both of us. This particular scoundrel will never again harm anyone," and with a sudden wrench he twisted the traitor's neck until there was a sharp *crack*. Tarzan tossed the limp body aside in casual disgust then went back up on deck, followed by Jane and Afya.

The battle above was over. Of the *Cowrie's* company, only Schmidt and Momulla and two others remained alive, having taken refuge in the main cabin. The others had died fitting deaths beneath the fangs and talons of the beasts of Tarzan.

Soon the morning sun rose on a second grisly scene on the deck of the unhappy *Cowrie*. This time, at least, the bloodstains on her white planking were those of the guilty.

Tarzan brought the men who had hidden in the main cabin onto the deck. They were offered no promise of immunity. Either they would help to sail the vessel, or he would put them to death immediately. They chose the only option that led to life.

A stiff breeze had risen with the sun. Under full sail the *Cowrie* set in toward Jungle Island. They arrived a short while later; Tarzan picked up Gust and said farewell to Sheeta and the apes of Akut, for here he set the beasts ashore to pursue the free life they loved so well. They wasted no time in disappearing into the cool depths of their beloved jungle. Only the more intelligent Akut remained on the beach, watching the small boat draw away toward the schooner where his savage master stood on the deck.

And as long as their eyes could span the distance, Jane and Tarzan stood on the deck watching the lonely figure of the shaggy ape, motionless on the surf-beaten sands of Jungle Island.

Three days later the *Cowrie* met *H.M.S. Shorewater*, a sloop-of-war of the Royal Navy. Using its wireless, Lord Greystoke soon contacted London. The news filled his and his wife's hearts with joy and thanksgiving—little Jack was safe at Lord Greystoke's townhouse. Only when they reached London did they learn the whole story.

Fearing to take the child aboard the *Kincaid* by day, Rokoff had hidden it in an orphanage for babies who had been abandoned. The plan was to carry it to the steamer after dark.

Paulvitch had learned a lot about treachery and greed from his wily master and had put those lessons to use. Lured by the thoughts of immense ransom, he had shared the secret with the woman running the orphanage. They had arranged for the substitution of another infant, knowing that Rokoff would never suspect the truth until it was too late.

The woman had promised to keep the boy until Paulvitch returned to England, but greed is contagious. She in turn had been tempted by the lure of gold and had opened negotiations with Lord Greystoke's attorneys for the return of the child.

Esmeralda, the elderly black American nurse, had been on vacation in Maryland when little Jack was abducted. When she returned and learned of the kidnapping, she was certain that only her absence had allowed it to happen in the first place—nor, seeing the fierce expression in her eyes, could anyone doubt the truth of her words. Happily for all, Esmeralda was able to positively identify the infant. The ransom had been paid, and within ten days of his kidnapping, the future Lord Greystoke was back at home, none the worse for his experience.

And so that last and greatest of Nikolai Rokoff's many crimes had not only failed miserably through the treachery of his one friend, but it had also resulted in the arch-villain's death. Lord and Lady Greystoke now enjoyed a peace of mind that neither could ever have felt so long as the Russian remained alive to cook up new atrocities for them.

As for Paulvitch, they had every reason to believe that the jungle had taken care of him. And so, they believed themselves forever free of the only two enemies Tarzan of the Apes had ever feared—not for his own sake, of course, but because they struck their cowardly blows mainly at those he loved.

It was a happy family party that were reunited in Greystoke House the day that Lord and Lady Greystoke landed on English soil from the deck of the *Shorewater*. Mugambi and Afya came with them; the young African woman much preferred the company of the chief of the Wagambi to the forcible marriage she had fled. Tarzan had invited them to live on his vast African estates in the land of the Waziri, where he would send them as soon as it could be arranged.

Possibly, we shall see them all there amid the savage romance of the grim jungle and the great plains where Tarzan of the Apes loves best to be.

Who knows?

AFTERWORD

About the Author

Everyone has heard of Tarzan, but few know much about his creator, one of the great pioneers of modern fiction: Edgar Rice Burroughs.

This adventure author's amazingly productive life can be divided neatly into halves: To use some images from *Tarzan*, Edgar Rice Burrough's first thirty-seven years were spent banging into one tree after another. But he spent his remaining thirty-eight years swinging through them with all the grace of his most famous literary creation.

Ed, as his family called him, was born into the comfortable middle-class family of George and Mary Evaline Burroughs in Chicago, Illinois on February 23, 1875, the youngest of four boys. George and Mary Evaline had married while George was a Union officer during the Civil War, and they were now highly respectable pillars of Chicago society. Ed's later actions would show his parents to be very patient and loving people.

Ed was a likable boy with a happy enough childhood. He was a bit of a troublemaker, but the constant flow of diseases through the school system in those days did far more harm to Ed's education than his inability to behave. In the late 1800s the flu was much deadlier than it is today, and Ed got sick often. Mr. and Mrs. Burroughs feared for their son's life in the crowded, polluted city, so when he was sixteen, they sent him packing to the brand-new state of Idaho to live a healthier life in the clean air of his uncle's cattle ranch.

It was a loving move, but a naïve one that they would soon regret. The adventuresome teen loved the rough-and-ready life of Idaho. The cowboys of 1891 were often gamblers, outlaws in hiding, or worse; and Ed had a fine time listening to their tall tales. Basically, Ed was a sixteen-year-old boy learning from men to get into man-sized trouble. His uncle did not protest, but his parents were another matter. Hanging around with shady characters and learning bad habits was not what they had in mind for their son, and they hurried him back to the Midwest.

Mr. and Mrs. Burroughs then tried sending their son to two different boarding schools, and the reports on his wild behavior only increased their worries. In those days, wealthy people with bad-boy sons often sent their sons away to private military schools for straightening out. Accordingly, in early 1892 Ed was packed off to the Michigan Military Academy for his high school education. That wasn't any help either. While Ed liked the idea of military life, it had too many rules and regulations, many of which he broke. As a cadet, he rose in rank only to find himself in trouble again. He was good at football and popular with his peers, but that did not help his grades and his behavior, which ranged from mediocre to bad. Only his father's influence enabled Ed to graduate.

After graduation, Ed taught briefly at the academy. It hardly suited his taste for adventure, and he soon joined the United States Cavalry. He was sent to the then-Arizona Territory in 1896 and discovered that peacetime Army life was mostly about manual labor. He hoped to become an officer, but his tendency toward poor health dictated otherwise, and he was discharged in 1897.

For the next three years, Ed went from art school in Chicago to his uncle's ranch to running a small business in Idaho. Then, after ten years of turning down his proposals, in 1900 his childhood sweetheart Emma Hurlbert agreed to marry him; they eventually had two sons and a daughter together. For the next twelve years, the future giant of fiction and his family barely managed to scrape by. At one point, they had to pawn Emma's jewelry to buy food. Ed bounced from job to job during that time, from office manager to railroad policeman to salesman, and he even applied without success to become an officer in the Chinese Army. While borrowing money to pay rent and feed his family, Ed could not have imagined what a different future awaited him.

In 1910, Ed made a cynical but practical decision. Having read a lot of 'pulp fiction'—typically
romances, westerns, and other action-packed writing not generally considered literature—he decided he could write similar stories. In 1911 Edgar
Rice Burroughs sold his first written work, intro-
ducing John Carter as the hero of *Under the Moons
of Mars*. This led to a series of adventures now
considered science fiction classics. Burroughs had
finally found his calling.

Shortly thereafter, in 1912, Burroughs sold
Tarzan of the Apes to a magazine for $700. It was
published in book form in 1914 and soon sold
over a million copies—a remarkable number for
the times. Burroughs went on to write a total of
twenty-six books about the ape-man. They succeeded beyond his wildest expectations, and they
capture readers' imagination to this day.

We can probably thank Hollywood for some
of Tarzan's popularity. Not everyone knew how to
read a book, but almost anyone could go to a
movie, even if they could not read the subtitles. In
1918, when movies were still silent, the first
Tarzan film was produced. When the Olympic
swimming hero Johnny Weissmuller began to play
the ape-man in 1932, and sound was added to
movies, Tarzan became what Luke Skywalker or
Indiana Jones would later become: not merely a
hero, but a household name.

No one seemed more surprised by his success than Burroughs himself. He was a refreshingly candid man who disliked bragging. In his own words: "I have been successful probably because I have always realized that I knew nothing about writing and have merely tried to tell an interesting story entertainingly."

Burroughs's later life included a divorce and remarriage, a stint as a town mayor, and the purchase of a California ranch called "Tarzana," which in 1928 became the name of a town that thrives to this day. Burroughs was playing tennis with his son in Hawaii on December 7, 1941, when the smoke began to rise from the bombing of Pearl Harbor by Japan. At 66, he was too old to enlist in the Army, but not too old for adventure; he went to work as a war correspondent, and even flew along on bombing missions with the Army Air Corps.

Edgar Rice Burroughs passed away in 1950 of a heart ailment; fittingly, he was reading a comic book in bed at the time.

His greatest adventure hero, Tarzan of the Apes, lives on, probably for generations yet to come.

About *The Beasts of Tarzan*

The Beasts of Tarzan is the third book in Edgar Rice Burroughs' series of twenty-six books about the ape-man. When it was first published in 1916, its success equaled that of the first two Tarzan books. For almost a hundred years, the popularity of the series has continued. What can explain such long-running interest in these books? In part, the stories have been kept alive by the popularity of Tarzan in other media; there are Tarzan movies, Tarzan television series, Tarzan cartoons, Tarzan games, and Tarzan comic books. But it is not just because of these things that people have continued to read the books. A closer look at some of the ingredients in *The Beasts of Tarzan* can help us understand its enduring popularity.

Part of the book's appeal is the exciting action. There is hardly a chapter that does not have at least one action scene. The kidnapping of little Jack in the first chapter is just a warm-up. By Chapter 3, Tarzan is sinking "his strong, white teeth . . . into the hairy throat" of the ape-king whom he must kill to save his own life. A bomb explodes and sinks the *Kincaid*; Mugambi, Akut, and Sheeta race along the banks of the Ugambi River to help Tarzan catch Rokoff; Jane fights off Rokoff and his dangerous crew; Rokoff is torn apart by Sheeta; Tarzan battles lions, crocodiles, apes, and African warriors. Open the book to almost any page and you'll find an action scene. It is nearly impossible not to be captivated by these powerful scenes.

But action scenes alone are not enough to explain the continuing popularity of *The Beasts of Tarzan*. Another important ingredient is the suspense that Burroughs builds into the book. One way he does this is by cutting away from a dramatic scene just before we find out what happens. Scenes like this are called cliffhangers. Chapter 1 ends with Tarzan locked in a little compartment onboard the *Kincaid* and hearing the scream of a frightened woman. Who is screaming? Why is she screaming? Where is Tarzan being taken? What will happen to him? The only way to find out is to read Chapter 2. This chapter ends with Tarzan stranded on the beach of Jungle Island. As he stares at the disappearing ship wondering what will happen to his son, "the hairy thing [is] creeping stealthily toward him." Will he turn around in time? Will he be able to fight off the creature? Who could possibly stop reading here?

In addition to using cliffhangers to keep the suspense high, Burroughs sets up long-running situations that keep us wondering and guessing. In Chapter 2 we see Jane trapped onboard the *Kincaid* by Rokoff. For the next six chapters we are left wondering what has happened to her. Burroughs keeps teasing us—and Tarzan—with bits of information. A woman and a child have been seen traveling up the Ugambi River. Is it Jane and Jack? But who is the man with them? Not until Chapter 9 do we find out what has happened. Burroughs even creates a suspenseful situation that continues throughout the entire book. In Chapter 1, Jack is kidnapped, but it is not until the final chapter of the book that we find out what happened to the child. The suspense keeps generations of readers coming back for more.

But the characters are just as important as the action and suspense in making the book engaging for today's readers. Jane demonstrates a strength, courage, and resourcefulness that we have to admire. Even when she believes Tarzan is dead, she does not give up. She fights off Rokoff and escapes into the dangerous jungle. When she gets to the canoe, she again drives Rokoff away. As she floats downstream, she keeps the canoe in the swiftest part of the river to make sure the Russian does not catch up with her. Once she gets onto the *Kincaid*, she fights off Rokoff a third time and then devises a plan that she hopes will get her back to London someday. She is clearly a determined woman.

Tarzan's heroic qualities also make the book appealing. His strength and resourcefulness are admirable. His goodness and his courage are highlighted by their sharp contrast to Rokoff's evil and cowardice. What's more, Tarzan is a character who represents the best of both the mental and the physical sides of human beings. He is highly intelligent—he taught himself to read, he speaks at least three human languages and various animal languages. And he is incredibly strong. He is the perfect blend of mental and physical strength. But most important of all is the integrity that he demonstrates through his words and his actions. He does not kill for pleasure—only for survival. He shows this in Chapter 3 when he tries to talk Akut out of fighting him; and, even though he cannot avoid the fight, he finally convinces Akut to surrender rather than be killed. A short while later, he saves Akut's life, further gaining the respect of the animal. Similarly, he saves Sheeta's life. And he spares Mugambi's life, an act that ultimately leads to a strong bond of friendship and respect between the two men. As Burroughs has shown in the previous two Tarzan books, the ape-man continues to be a man of principle who is intent on doing the right thing.

These ingredients—action, suspense, admirable characters—continue to engage readers nearly a hundred years after they were written. Burroughs makes us experience the excitement of the action and the tension of the suspense. He shows us what it means to be a human being whose actions come from his principles and his integrity. Because of these qualities, the books are timeless stories to read.